VENEFICIA PUBLISHING UK
https://www.veneficiapublishing.com
Typesetting © Veneficia Publishing UK July 2019

CONTENTS

Because of the cosmopolitan nature of this book, it features contributions written in both American English and British English

IMAGE CONTENTS

INTRODUCTION

There are several worlds, all of which are intertwined with this world, the world we live in day to day; the mundane reality. However, each turn of a tarot card opens a portal to another world; a potential future world yet to be experienced. Many of us seek out fortune tellers, card readers and those considered blessed with the gift to unlock these secret worlds and offer us an insight into our potential futures. And those who shuffle and cut the cards are the inquirers; the seekers of their own destiny. Most commonly, they are searching for answers to matters of the heart, or health and finances.

Each Tarot deck consists of the major and minor arcana. The major arcana consists of 22 cards numbered from 0-XXI, containing often elaborate and beautiful images. When spread out in numerical order they tell the Fool's journey with each card metaphorically depicting a stage of life. By shuffling and cutting the cards, the inquirer puts their energy into the cards while focussing on the question they are seeking answers too.

With a simple turn of the cards the reader offers a glimpse into the inquirer's future...for a price of course.

Featuring writers from various continents, this book tells the fictitious stories of just some of the many potential worlds that lay behind each of the major arcana. Some, but not all the writers are tarot readers; but we will leave it up to you to decide which ones are and which ones aren't. Either way the intention is to entertain, intrigue and amuse.

0 THE FOOL

THE FOOL
Jane; A Fools Journey - Diane Narraway

My name is Jane, although these days I am known as "Jane the Foole." I am what they call an innocent. Innocent! That would be funny if it wasn't so tragic. My story begins on a small tied island off the coast of Britain and whether I am a fool or not is up to you to decide.

It was always said that there was something "different" about me. I couldn't stay still, was easily distracted and often blurted out my view of life, whether it was required or not and because of this I was not required to work. Something about being a danger to others and myself, getting in the way or not being trusted to do simple tasks were some of the many reasons I had been given.

Either way I had become unemployable, and if you couldn't work, heal or predict the future, you were an unproductive member of society, and of course reliant on your family's income.

Life was harsh for everyone and my family couldn't realistically afford an extra mouth to feed that was unable to contribute, and although they struggled, for the most part, I was safe, warm and didn't go hungry. I wouldn't say that I was loved but my basic needs were met, or at least they were until one day, without warning I was thrown out or "asked to leave" as they put it - It all amounted to the same thing, I was homeless; a beggar and as such dependant on the kindness of others. I'm not sure why I was thrown out, but while the rest of the village mourned the passing of the parish priest; the only man who ever treated me with any kindness, I became homeless and hungry. Admittedly a few of the women would hand me a crust here and there but the men, well, that's another story. Innocent is how they refer to me yet there were several men in my village who of made sure I was far from that.

2

There are just some things you never forget. As soon as I was old enough to bear children it was as if they could smell it on me and maybe they could.

I remember the first time…

I was trying to sleep in an out-building one cold night when two of the quarry men passed by. I heard them talking and like the fool they thought I was I asked if they had any food; I was cold and hadn't eaten all day. They came close, I could smell the ale on their breath and the look in their eyes unnerved me. I wasn't sure what it meant but I didn't feel at ease with it, and rightly so! Although the rest is a bit of a hazy blur, I remember their hot breath on my face as they tugged at my skirts one after the other, but most of all I remember the pain.

Word must have got around because after that I seemed to be the village whore except, I would be "lucky" to get anything in exchange. Occasionally, and I mean very occasionally I might get a crust of bread or a drink "for my trouble." It wasn't so much trouble as it was hell! So, between the taunts of the children, the harsh words from bitter wives and the nightly visits from drunks and gandermooners,[1] all of which were a far cry from the love bards wrote or sang about, food was scarce and human compassion virtually non-existent.

One night, everything changed, it was bitterly cold in the outhouse where I had sought shelter; I varied where I slept but it never mattered someone always found me.

There was no sanctuary. They say no door is ever locked to a fool but what the law says and what really happens are two very different things, and even those unlocked doors carry a price.

On this occasion a man "seeking my company" as he put it, was particularly brutal, leaving me almost for dead; tossing me a stale crust as he left me there sobbing in the dirt. I had no tears left to cry, so I just lay there sobbing, every inch of me hurting unable to move; partially through hunger but mostly through pain. I have no idea how long I was there, but I must have eventually fallen asleep as the cold wintry sunlight streaming in through the gap in the door woke me. Stretching, I could feel the warmth of another body next to me, and I was almost afraid to look, but curiosity as always got the better of me.

A small dog had curled up beside me, presumably he too was cold, probably hungry, and I'll wager "far too used" to being on the end of someone's boot. I shared the stale crust of bread I had *earned* the night before with him and for the first time in forever I felt genuine affection.

I had spent the day begging with the little dog beside me and I shared any of the meagre scraps I was given with him. It felt good having someone else to care for, and it gave me the strength to leave the village and take my chances elsewhere. This was not a decision I had made lightly. Obviously, I had considered running away many times, who wouldn't, but the law was such that anyone caught leaving their village to seek work elsewhere was to be whipped through the streets as a vagabond. I could not apply to the JP[2] as although my home village had deemed me too stupid to work, I had no obvious physical disabilities and would likely be whipped as a lubberwort;[3] my options were limited to say the least. Stay here and put up with the nightly visits or take my chances as a vagabond.

Once the sun had set and before the menfolk came to seek me out, me and the little dog made our way tentatively along the treacherous coastal paths. It was a cold February evening and the wind whipped at my face and hands. The rags I was dressed in and had been for months kept little of the icy cold out; my tiny frame stung with the cold. We made our way along the west cliff path; it was well trodden, but the ground was wet and slippery. The wind was so icy cold it burned, and the salt spray from the cold-hearted ocean which beckoned below bit hard into my frozen face. In truth, I wasn't sure we'd make it off the island let alone find a better life but going back wasn't an option.

4

It wasn't a long walk to the mainland, an able-bodied farm hand could walk it in a couple of hours but for a poorly dressed, half-starved and very tired young girl accompanied by an equally thin and tired small dog it was a long walk.

In fact, the morning star rose before we'd reached the tied beach and we were forced to spend the daylight hidden in one of the few crevices large enough to accommodate us; waif and stray that we were.

It took us a couple of days on our coastal journey before we were forced to stop and ask for food, by which time we had reached Abbotsbury and I knew that whichever door we knocked upon it was going to cost me, but both me and the little dog were physically exhausted, painfully thin and I could feel death growing ever closer. Probably more for the little dog than myself I made the decision to ask for food. I could see the Abbey up ahead and decided that was possibly our best option. I didn't for one moment think it would cost me any less, my reasoning was simply that Abbeys had more money than your average household and we badly needed food and sleep.

The Abbey itself was daunting, far larger than even the castle back home, or where home would have been had I had one. I knocked on the huge wooden door and my heart pounded in my chest as I waited for a response. After what seemed an eternity, a monk finally opened a smaller door within the large wooden door and beckoned me to enter. He didn't ask what I wanted, why would he? It was obvious to anyone that I was emaciated and on the brink of collapsing for the final time. I had been hungry before and had become accustomed to exhaustion; I'd felt it often enough, but this was, a new sensation and I could feel death's icy grip tightening with every breath.

He sat me down and fetched a bowl of broth and the Prior. 'Fetch some scraps for the dog too,' another man, who I presumed was the prior ordered the monk, as he watched me trying to share the broth with the little dog. Once I had eaten the few mouthfuls

I could manage, the Prior requested I be taken to the infirmary along with my dog. I had never seen him as *my* dog, just another poor wretch like me who desperately needed a friend. He ordered I be left to rest and sure enough I was that first night, the second night was different though.

I had been fed and rested and fed again and my stomach actually, felt full, and me and the little dog were beginning to feel safe. But once again, I was awoken late at night by a group of monks; three possibly four, it was hard to tell in the dark. They were just shadows around my bed, but I knew all too well their intention.

I had almost resigned myself to the fact that I must pay for their kindness in the usual fashion when the Prior entered the room and shooed them all out. I could hear them outside the infirmary. The Prior sounded firm in his instructions.

'Leave her be! She is only a child and a poorly nourished one at that! She needs our compassion and care. Hospitality, not further heartache!' There was a pause before adding '... And the same goes for her dog. There are plenty enough bawds and whores around. Cool your lust with them, not a beggar girl!'

"Beggar girl." That's what he called me, I cried real tears at those words; at what I had become. I was just 13 years old and all I'd known was indifference, cruelty and hunger.

The Prior was called Roger and he was a kind, gentle man, who took me in and nursed me back to health, and who once I was healthy taught me to read and write, cook, farm and mend clothes. Both me and the little dog were safe and well cared for. But, like all things, this idyllic life was destined to end less than a year later.

The King had ordered that the monastery be surrendered, and Roger knew it was a case of give in gracefully and accept the pension. I had heard talk of monasteries closing, being dismantled and their stone being used to build castles or other fortifications.

6

Something to do with the Kings divorce, but I didn't really need to understand anything beyond the fact that I was likely to be homeless again. I for one, was saddened by the news as it looked as though I would return to the streets, and become a *beggar girl* again, but Roger with his kind gentle eyes and soft voice tried to reassure me that this would not be the case; that he would find somewhere for me to live.

I didn't see how as life was hard for the average household and my skills, while they were more than they had been, were limited. They were certainly not good enough for me to go into service, so I began hoarding what I could, which truth to tell was also limited; bits of cheese or salted meat for as long as it would last.

I remember my final days there vividly. Amidst the chaos of inquiries, finger pointing and arrests, Roger remained resolute in his defence and was spared any further accusation by a knock at the door from a very well to do man; he had come to get me. Sir Giles, and in "not so hushed whispers" I learned that the monks had looked after his favourite mistress when she went down with childbed fever, back last year, after having his bastard. Roger had also found a home for the child and was now calling in the favour. He was to find me lodgings. Sir Giles had connections up country, and both me and the little dog would be safe with him and well looked after.

Sir Giles also had an eye for a pretty girl and made many lewd remarks as we rode; I didn't feel safe at all, in fact I felt right back where I started. This time was different though, both me and the dog were healthier and stronger, and the dog could sense my fear and snarled baring his teeth and so, Sir Giles kept his distance. Still, I suspected it was only a matter of time.

As we travelled, the sound of thundering hooves could be heard coming towards us. It was a carriage with a crest on the side. I had never seen anything like it before and we must have looked pretty peculiar; Sir Giles perched atop his grey mare and me walking along behind with my belongings, such as they were and the little dog trotting along behind me. A man's voice called to the driver and both they and us stopped. A woman peered out of the carriage.

My saviour, captor, call him what you will, announced himself,

'Sir Giles at your service Ma'am.'

'You are a knight of the realm?' came a posh voice from inside the coach.

'Some knight…I thought knights were meant to be chivalrous' I blurted out, followed by quickly slapping my hands over my mouth but all too late, the lady in the carriage had already heard me.

She laughed 'And what's your name young lady…might I ask?'

'Jane Ma'am' I thought that must be the right address as Sir Giles the unchivalrous had used it.

'Jane what?'

I had absolutely no idea if I had a surname or not, so I used the only name I'd ever been called.

'Beg pardon Ma'am, I believe it's Jane the fool.'

She laughed 'How funny, we'll take her won't we,' directing the question to her fellow traveller, presumably the man whose voice I'd heard earlier.

'She can be a wedding gift.'

He must've agreed as she beckoned me closer.

'I've never been a gift before…is the little dog to be a gift too?' I gazed down towards the small black dog beside me.

'Of course.' She smiled, opening the carriage door, gesturing for us to join her, and the faceless male voice in the carriage. The year was 1535 and while it was another few years before the monastery actually closed, one way or another, me and the little dog had not returned to the streets.

The lady who had taken a shine to me was none other than the Queen, and the faceless voice King Henry, heading home after one of their progresses. Not only had this fortuitous meeting saved me from Sir Giles unwelcome advances and potentially a return to vagrancy, but it also led to me meeting one of the kindest and cleverest men I had ever known: Will Somers.

His eyes always shone mischievously; like he knew a secret. For me it was love at first sight and the more we got to know each other the more in love with him I fell, we were soon married although we never had children. I suspect years of hunger and brutality had taken its toll on my ability to have children.

I was privy to the Queen's chamber and she consulted me on many things and always said that I was the wisest fool she knew. Like all things in my life this was not to last, as she was executed only a year later. I cried real tears at the time, and I will never forget her. She had seen something in me that even my family hadn't seen. And through her I became a wife, an adviser and would go on to be the wise fool to all those queens who succeeded her. I Jane the Foole; I Jane Somers

---

1 In Tudor English, a gandermooner was a man who flirted with other women while his wife recovered from childbirth.

2 In Tudor England, Justices of the Peace (JPs) were the chief local government officers, appointed by the King and responsible for keeping law and order in their area.

3 Lubberwort was a 16th Century name of an imaginary plant that allegedly caused sluggishness or stupidity; ultimately becoming used as a nickname for a lethargic or fuzzy-minded person.

Magus

I THE MAGICIAN

THE MAGICIAN
Where Paradigms Conjoin - Geraldine Lambert

The Magician sat in her scruffy torn armchair thinking aloud whilst looking through the window at the dropped petals of the hellebore. Their cream blossom, once shining like a star in the cold airs of winter were now tipped with the bronzing of decay.

The spring held new promises and life was becoming easier since developing an understanding with her significant and sacred Holy Guardian Spirit. New mental agility gave strength and power to her recent workings and magical pastimes. She had arranged and charted a couple of 'lucky stars,' a sigil of Jupiter; a call to Sachiel to help an old friend, and a token for renewed perseverance and substance for a stranger. Tonight, she would call for new luck for herself. Weakened of spirit following illness during the winter, she needed to bring forth her innate Will and relate its power with the conjuration within her subconscious mind.

She required the favour of Raphael/Thoth to bring increase and growth to her magical formula. She would wear her robes of liquid fabrics in the colours of yellow hue. Enhanced by the power of Air, the cloth would ripple and shimmer within the light.

She also sought the daunting powers of Uriel to bring a sublime haste to her enchantments. She thus entwined the colours of plant, ribbon and ragged loose thread to weave a spectrum of correspondences and old powers together. An 'electric bluebell' and a pouty bright marigold hybrid would stand in for Uranus and Michael. Green laurel leaves from a hedge and then off to the woods where early cream blossom bloomed alone upon a thorn. A pinch of yellow from a primrose by the roadside would suffice for the power of Mercury, and the illuminated Periwinkle would represent Jupiter's royal purple. Silver seed pods of Honesty would represent her beloved Lady Moon and Gabriel.

This wild bouquet with its colourful correspondences of the Sacred Powers was made complete with an early crimson tulip that sat in a pot bathed in sunlight. Ares and Samael would be pleased with such a specimen of fiery red, upright and phallic in its stance. She tied the plants together with multi coloured thread and placed them ready by the window side.

That evening she stood in the wildland with her cup and four candles alight with their yellow flames, her black kitchen knife now laid by the side of the 'old man' wand. The hue of the plants and richly coloured threads kept her 'tools of force' company on a grey slate stand. With firm stance she stood astride to pull the strength of direction and juggle the Powers to her Will. Calling with confidence and composure whilst using the force of vibration within the air, she made her request to the designated Spirits.

She recalled the old code; To Know, To Will, To Dare, To Keep Silent. Both strength and humility were balanced with dignity and might. Her toes wet with sodden mud as her speech emphasized the dare of her requisition - she stood small and robed as the stars watched, whilst the moon spied. Twinkles of rain joined the Rite with spits of inconvenient kisses. With a heart of fire that leapt as the candle flame flickered, the elongated shadows within the nightshade bobbed with facial contours.

Energy crawled her spine, rapture caught her eye, and whispers tricked her breath...

Then silence.

The scent of nature and a saturation of electricity stood heavy within the night.

Passively she folded her robe and tied its cord into a package withholding her tools of trade.

Back home, alone, she knew herself not to speak. She never spoke to anyone about the rites she performed beneath sun and moon and the corresponding hours. No one knew of her inner plight of symbolic conversations with the Watchers. Forever with her, they would observe, listen, challenge and guide. Their aid was always gratefully received but their obstacles set into her fate, she thought, quite tricky at times.

These were, after all, the uneasy relentless afflictions an initiate had to bear and overcome. She saw it as a process of breaking the spirit, and then training the mind to set the Will and to exchange its energy to wield and direct occult power. The Magician comprehended the skill of thought to adapt and revise change.

She knew stealthily she would overcome the courts of Lady Fortuna with her ever-revising trials of loss and increase.

However, to experience is to know, and gnosis enables growth, and expansion matures into adeptship. To seek the lore of power, and to comprehend the love of the archetype, is a means to gain a piece of the sphere of advantageous possibility, where paradigms conjoin.

II THE HIGH PRIESTESS

THE HIGH PRIESTESS

Mojo Bag - Laurie Pneumatikos

Heka was sitting in her kitchen table enjoying a cup of tea. It was a bright, sunny morning and the birds were singing. She had opened all the windows in the small apartment behind the shop and the sweet scent of honeysuckle and mimosa wafted in with the cool breeze. She relished these moments when the earth was vibrant with life. Soon she would be busy harvesting various fruits, herbs and roots from her gardens and preparing them for the year ahead.

She rinsed her cup, placed it in the rack and put her shoes on to go outside and water the plants when the bell on the shop door rang. When she stepped through the door separating her small apartment from the shop, she saw a confused looking young Hispanic woman holding a baby.

"Hello dear! What can I do for you?"

The young woman stammered, "I, uh… My baby. She's really sick. The doctors said there's nothing more they can do." Tears began streaming down her red, swollen cheeks. "Mama G told me to bring her here. She said you have powerful medicines."

Heka reached out a hand, "I'm Heka. What is your name my dear?"

"I'm sorry! I am Consuela and this is Alicia."

"Very good! Follow me." Heka said as she led the young woman through the beaded curtain into a small room and motioned for her to place the baby on the examination table.

She lifted the small cloth, the baby girl was staring lethargically, and Heka could see that she was dying. Heka placed her left hand on the baby's forehead and closed her eyes, muttering the names of ancient gods. The young mother felt a powerful wave of energy surge through the room and she began to shake uncontrollably. She felt as if something was pushing her back and

15

she landed in a nearby chair. The moment she connected with the chair, a sense of calm took over and she watched as Heka picked up the baby and carried her in her arms while dancing and chanting.

The young mother watched as a colourful whirlwind appeared and began to swirl around them growing and flowing into the baby. Then there was a loud whoosh and it was all over. The room was silent again and Heka was standing in front of her staring down at the baby as she began to whimper, then cry.

Heka handed the baby back to her mother and the young woman followed her back into the shop where Heka busily retrieved glass jars from the shelves and placed them on the counter. Then she retrieved a small cloth bag and began filling it with herbs from the jars. "You are breastfeeding her still?"

"Yes Ma'am."

Heka tied off the bag and placed it in a tea pot.

"Sit down over there." Heka motioned for her to sit at one of the tables while she poured hot water over the bag, placed the lid on the pot and retrieved a cup and saucer from the cupboard. She placed all of it on a tray with the pot and carried the tray to the table. "We will give it a few minutes to steep before we pour."

Heka pulled another cloth bag from the drawer, a larger one; and began filling it with different herbs. When the bag was full, she tied it off in a triple knot and handed it to the young woman. "When you get home, put this in the baby's cot and leave it there for 7 days and 7 nights. It will turn black and then you must bring it back to me. You must not delay in returning the bag to me. Do you understand?"

"Yes ma'am."

The young mother accepted the bag from Heka as the baby started to whimper again. She thanked her and Heka gave her a stern look. "You MUST return the bag after 7 days and 7 nights. Do not delay or the baby will get sick again! Promise me!"

"I won't. I promise!" The young mother put the cloth bag

16

in her purse, took out a battered wallet and poured its meagre contents onto the counter.

"I'm sorry. This is all I have. But I have chickens and I can bring you eggs. I also make tapestries and sell them on the corner. I will bring you one."

"That will be fine. You bring me the tapestry and 13 eggs when you bring back the bag. But you keep your money. You will need it to feed your baby and make her strong again."

The young woman tearfully thanked her as Heka poured the tea into the cup. "Do you take honey in your tea?"

"No" said the young woman.

Heka told her to drink all of it; including the tea in the pot.

After the young woman left, Heka went out and communed with the garden spirits as she watered. The sun was warm, the earth was cool, and the flowers were in full bloom. She gently harvested some of the delicate flowers and leaves for her medicine room, thanked the spirits for her bounty, then went inside and washed up.

As she placed a pot of soup on the stove, she heard the bell over the shop door once again.

There was a distinguished gentleman waiting. He was tall and black as coal, and when he spoke, his baritone voice and Jamaican accent was melodious and soothing. He used an old cane when he walked and the top of it had a serpent's head made of carved ivory. He gallantly removed his hat and bowed ever so subtly, "Good morning Madam!"

"Good morning Dear Sir! What can I do for you this fine day?"

"I have need of a few things for my work" the distinguished gentleman said. "I was told that you may be able to help me obtain these items." The gentleman stepped forward and handed her a lovely piece of parchment paper with a precisely printed list. She scanned it, then looked up into his eyes, and he was quite taken aback by her penetrating gaze. She too, nearly lost her sense of balance when she looked into his dark, intense eyes. She caught herself and he smiled as a thin blue arc formed in the air connecting them.

Her nearly imperceptible nod signaled that she understood.

"I have most of these. But the toads have not matured yet and the leeches won't be delivered until next Wednesday. The bat's wool, nightshade and calamus root were harvested last year but the bloodroot is fresh, and the newts are young and lively."

"Very good Madam! I will take what you have if you be willing."

"Would you be coming back this way next week for the remaining items or are you passing through? I can put the leeches and toads aside for you next week if you like Sir."

"That would be excellent Madam! How much do I owe you for all of it? I shall be here next week to retrieve the rest of it."

"Well, the leeches have been fetching a higher price these days and…"

"Madam" he interrupted, "Will this cover it?" He pulled five crisp $100 bills out of his black leather wallet and laid them down on the counter.

Heka glanced down, and seeing they were real, swept them up and placed them in her pocket. She looked into the tall man's eyes. "Yes, this will cover it. Please be seated while I assemble your order Sir. Would you like a cup of tea?"

"Yes Madam. That would be delightful!"

Heka brought the kettle in from the kitchen and retrieved the small porcelain pot and delicate china cup from the cupboard. She filled a muslin bag with aromatic spices and black tea before tying it off and pouring the water. She retrieved a jug of fresh cream from the small refrigerator under the counter and added a homemade biscuit on a saucer before carrying the tray over to his table. The biscuit was a special recipe, reserved for special guests.

When she set the tray down on the table in front of the

gentleman, his senses were overwhelmed with the fresh, almost intoxicating fragrances.

She quickly retreated to the back patio where she stored the live critters and came back with a glass jar full of newts.

The tall gentleman watched her as she busily retrieved jars and began filling bags with roots and herbs. She retrieved the bat's wool from under the counter, filled a large bag, and placed everything in a box.

The tall man carefully wrapped the biscuit in one of the napkins she provided and put it in his pocket before he jumped up with a wide grin on his face and thanked Heka as she carried the box over to him. When he reached out to grasp the box, his fingers gently brushed her hand and their eyes met. Something more than the box passed between them and Heka felt a twinge of fluttering in her chest. Her voice nearly faltered as she thanked him back, but she managed to get past it without embarrassing herself. He tipped his hat as he said, "I'll see you next week then, Madam!"

Heka watched him go out the door, then she ran to the window to see which direction he went, perhaps she would see what he was driving, but…nothing. Nobody was there. It was as if he had disappeared the moment he stepped out. When she turned back around, she saw that he had left a card on the table.

Thomas Legba, Legba Enterprises
Speak Thrice at the Crossroads

Heka was intrigued by the cryptic message. It was unlike any business card she had ever seen. There was no phone number and no address.

She placed the card in her pocket, intending to return to her chores when the door opened again. It was an elderly man with an unsteady gait but used no cane or walker. Heka held her breath as she watched him stagger toward her, praying he would not fall.

"Good afternoon Sir! What can I help you with this afternoon?"

"Are you the proprietor?"

"Yes sir, I am!"

"It's my wife. Our son died last month and now she won't eat or sleep. She cries all the time and she has lost so much weight that I'm afraid she will wither away and die. A neighbor told me to come and see you. He said you may be able to help my wife."

"I'm sorry for your loss, sir. How did your son pass?" "He was a drug addict. He stole almost everything we had to buy his drugs. He even stole my wife's jewelry. And worse, he yelled at her and threatened her and made her cry when we had no more for him to steal. Then he broke into a neighbor's house and the neighbor shot him. Now my wife is inconsolable. If she dies, I will die of a broken heart as well. Can you help me? I'm afraid all I have to offer you is my old stamp collection I kept hidden in the attic. It is worth a little money, I think."

"Yes, that will do. I can help you. What is your wife's name?"

"Myra."

"Okay Sir, please sit over there while I put a together some herbs."

As before, Heka retrieved some jars from the shelves and began placing a pinch of this and a dash of that into a cloth bag, tying it off when finished and handing it to the sad elderly man. "Take this bag and place it under your wife's side of the mattress for seven days and seven nights. It will turn black during that time. After seven days and seven nights, you must return this bag to me. Do you understand?"

"Yes. I must return the bag after seven days and seven nights."

"Don't forget! If you don't return the bag to me, your wife will get worse! It is crucial that you return it to me! You may bring the stamp collection when you return the bag. Okay?"

She held out the bag and he took it gratefully, "Yes, I will! Thank you!"

The man left and not five minutes later, a woman came in with her young son as Heka was wiping down the counter. Heka recognized her. Her son was being bullied by the other kids in school. One of the bullies, an older boy they called Billy, had beat the so badly that he had been in a coma at the local hospital.

His mother had come to see Heka previously, in tears, begging her to help her son.

"Hello Miss Tegan! Did you bring me the bag?"

"Yes, it's in my purse!" The woman fought back tears expressing her gratitude as she set down a large shopping bag and dug through her purse. "This is my boy Jamison. He is well now, thanks to you! The doctors said he was probably not going to wake up, and if he did wake up, that he would be blind. I put the little bag in the bed with him, and three days later he woke up blind, but his sight returned a few days after that! They say it was a miracle!"

Heka reached out and the boy flinched. "No worries my dear. Come here and let me touch your head."

"Go on son," Ms. Teagan said. "Let her touch you."

The boy closed his eyes as Heka touched his forehead, muttering something unintelligible under her breath as she lay hands on the boy. "Jamison, they will never touch you again my dear. You are a mirror now. Whatever they try to do to you will reflect onto them. If they are kind to you, they will be treated kindly. And if they try to harm you, they will be harmed before they can touch you. You will never have reason to fear again."

Heka turned to the boy's mother who was holding the black bag by the string. Heka produced a small paper sack from her pocket, opened it, and motioned for her to drop it in. She closed the bag immediately, walked over to a salt statue of Simbi, lifted the head and dropped the bag inside. The boy's mother picked up the large shopping bag and held it out to Heka.

Heka looked inside: turnips, ginger, parsley, and a lovely purple, pink and green shawl. "My grandmother knitted the shawl for me before she passed. She would want you to have it. The other things are from my garden."

"It's very beautiful! Thank you." Heka was pleased to have something so pretty to wear during the winter months.

As soon as the door gently clicked behind them, the phone rang.

"Miss Heka's Tea shop. May I help you?"

"Miss Heka?"

"Yes."

"This is Charles Kemp. I saw you about three weeks ago about my brother. He was in an accident. Do you remember me?"

"Yes, I remember you Mr. Kemp."

"My brother woke up after 7 days, and he was doing really well for a few days. But then he got real sick again. He died last night so your medicine bag clearly didn't work."

"I'm sorry for your loss Mr. Kemp. But you did not return the bag to me after seven days and seven nights as instructed."

"What does that matter? That old thing turned black like you said it would and I threw it away! Why would you want it back?"

"Mr. Kemp, it hurts me to hear that your brother passed, but I instructed you to bring the bag back to me after seven days and seven nights. That was the agreement. Since you didn't follow through with our agreement, your brother, tragically, relapsed. I am sorry for your loss."

"But why would that kill my brother?"

"Mr. Kemp, did you place the bag in a trash bin in the home or outside of the home?"

"I threw it in the trash basket in his bedroom. What difference does it make?"

"Is it still there?"

"I don't know...maybe...why should it matter?"

"Mr. Kemp. I'm sorry. There is nothing more I can do for you." Heka gently laid the phone down, cutting him off. She was distressed. 'He will no-doubt, look in that trash basket and find that the bag had turned white again.'

The bell to the shop door rang again and Heka looked up to see Momma G. coming in with a basket of goodies and a smile on her face. "I brought peaches, homemade bread and jelly today!"

"Great Momma! There's soup on the stove! A nice gentleman gave us a hambone yesterday!" Heka walked over to the door and turned the sign to closed as she locked it.

They sat at the table in the garden, surrounded by trees and flowers and butterflies. The sounds of the small fountains, chattering birds and the buzzing honeybees filled the air in this backyard paradise. The ice cubes clinked as Heka poured the warm tea over them and they chatted about the weather and their families back home.

After lunch, Heka turned the sign back around to say, 'Open for business' and unlocked the door.

It was a good day and she sold almost enough tea and mojo bags to pay the rent, but something was off. She took the business card that Mr. Legba left and placed it next to the register after rediscovering it in her pocket. But minutes later, she felt it in her pocket again as she was talking with a customer. At first, she thought it was a trick of her memory, perhaps she had intended to take it out and place it next to the register...maybe she had been distracted? So, she took it out of her pocket and placed it next to the cash register.

A few minutes later, as she was handing a package of tea to a customer, she looked down and spotted the business card peeking out of her pocket. She was alarmed, and this pestered her, but she was too busy to stop and analyze the how and why of it. She found herself fiddling with it in her pocket as she talked with customers, which she found even more disturbing because she felt like she was losing control. She was drawn to it somehow.

That night she made herself a cup of tea and warmed up some of the leftover soup. She had barely finished the soup before the exhaustion hit her hard. She was asleep the second her head hit the pillow.

But it didn't last. After two hours of restless sleep, Heka found herself walking down the dark alleys of the city. Only she wasn't really walking...she was gliding.

The night people were out and about; street venders selling the last of the day's hot dogs and tacos, drug dealers and ladies on the corners wearing short skirts and low-cut blouses offering their services to men in cars. She passed three men on a stoop sitting around a small hibachi grill that was covered with meat, they drank beer, laughed and chatted in Spanish. They did not notice her.

The traffic lights and the neon bar signs reflected the colors of the street, that danced in the mist as the steam rose from the pavement.

She didn't notice the light drizzle as she fiddled with the business card in her pocket.

The streets became dimmer and less populated as she floated past closed shops and darkened warehouses. She was alone in the stillness and the mist disappeared.

Suddenly realizing that she was no longer in the city, she stopped and looked around. She was surrounded by a field of wildflowers that were swaying in the cool breeze. Under the light of the full moon they ran the spectrum of grays and blues, and beyond them were dark patches of trees. She looked down and noticed that she was standing in the middle of a crossroad. The cool breeze felt good on her bare legs as it kicked up the hem of her dress. The wildflowers were glowing now; delicate shades of blue and green appeared, becoming brighter, some turning violet and pink. As she stood there in amazement, she felt a light touch. She knew who was touching her hand before she turned around and looked into his eyes.

24

Heka opened her eyes and stared at the ceiling fan above. In her mind's eye, she was still staring into his eyes when she heard a voice – HIS voice, "Come to the Crossroads my dear!" His voice echoed throughout the room, followed by laughter as it trailed off into the gentle whir of the ceiling fan.

After that, sleep did not come. Heka, shaken, got up and made herself a cup of chamomile tea. As she sat in the dim kitchen, she turned the business card over and over in her hand staring at the now glowing letters; first gold then green then red. Then the letters changed altogether.

COME TO THE CROSSROADS HEKA.

III THE EMPRESS

THE EMPRESS
The Debut - Diane Narraway

I always wanted children but it either wasn't the right time, or I wasn't in the right relationship, to be honest I was rarely in any relationship. The brief fling I'd had with Dan had ended almost as soon as it had started. I resigned myself to the fact that there were more than enough children in the world and that teaching them was the next best thing to having them, and at least I got to go home at night. My daily routine was pretty much the same with the odd night out or night in chatting with "Mr far from right" on a useless dating site, my friends had suggested I join. I am tempted at times to rethink my definition of friend!

Today will be different I thought to myself gazing at the tired primary school teacher that was looking back at me from the hallway mirror. My clothes were drab and ill-fitting at best, but my nails were long and had shone brilliantly in the sun walking back from the nail boutique. The nail technician, a strange phrase I feel, but that is their title had said I was lucky to get an appointment. I reinforced my affirmation that today, or at least what was left of it would be different. It had been a long week at work, but it wasn't a put your feet up night; I was grabbing tonight with both hands.

I prepared for the night ahead ritualistically, probably because I had mentally run through the "getting ready" process every night for the last month or so. I had laid in bed contemplating make-up techniques, praying that I didn't put on weight, that my hair complied and that nothing, and I mean nothing would go wrong.

Of course, I had practiced my make-up. I had tried on my dress, but I hadn't put the whole ensemble together. I wanted to wait, to enjoy the anticipation and indulge the excitement that comes with waiting. I had even chosen my evening meal carefully, in order to eat nothing that might cause indigestion, heartburn, wind or any other embarrassing bodily functions.

I savour every moment as the heady mixture of water, shower gel and hair conditioner trickle over my naked body; inhaling the different scents as they merge into one glorious aroma. The bathrobe feels soft and I am one step closer to tonight. I look at myself again, smiling at the schoolteacher looking back at me, this is where the night really begins.

I put on my hair cap. I look like I'm wearing a condom on my head and I can't help but smile. I must have watched a million make-up tutorials, learning as many tips and tricks as I can so as not to mess this up. And because tonight has the potential to be the best night of my life I have spared no expense on my paint box of foundations, concealers, highlighters, mascaras, eyeliners, powders, brushes and the myriad of eyeshadows and lip colours; all laid out before me now.

I begin unconventionally by using a brown eyeshadow applied with an angled brush to define my eyebrows. I have a scar on the brow line, a constant reminder of the last fight I had with Dan. Not that he'd caused it or anything, I had embarrassingly tried to prevent him from leaving and tripped over, smacking my head on the coffee table. This was not my proudest moment and one that had no business interrupting tonight's ritual. The hair doesn't grow there and so the best method to hide this, is eyeshadow. Within moments both Dan and his memory are wiped from my face.

Next the foundation, my skin is quite olive, or as Dan called it "dirty gypsy." Whatever you call it, it was the Devils own job finding a decent foundation to match it; not cheap either. I wondered whether I should have gone for the spray tan but, I only have so much money and on top of everything else it would have overstretched my finances. It already feels like most of my monthly salary has gone into looking my best tonight. I haven't skimped on anything else; only the best for tonight.

Slowly I apply the concealer, highlighting and accentuating the natural contours of my face while hiding the bags left over from the long nights marking year 2 SATS papers. I add a touch of highlighter under my bottom lip for a bit of extra pout and step by step I am becoming somebody far more glamorous than normal.

Once I have blended everything to my satisfaction, I dust with powder; the soft sable brush feels almost sensual as it drifts over my skin, adding a subtle glow.

They say the eyes are the windows to the soul, and therefore, the choice of colour is of paramount importance and I have chosen my colours a hundred times over before settling on pinks and silver to match my dress. Despite all this I am still tempted to consider other options, but after further deliberation I decide to stick with the pink and silver. Even as I put the colour on, I tingle with excitement and am in awe of my face as it slowly changes with every stroke of the brush.

Now for the only cheap part of my make-up kit, the black liquid eyeliner; a *Superdrug* special. I carefully paint it along the lid with an exaggerated flick at the end, before adding white liner inside the bottom lid. The latter makes my eyes look bigger, giving them that extra "je ne sais quoi."

I cannot believe how stunning I am starting to look; it is becoming harder and harder to recognise myself. I have waited a long time for this and everything about it needs to be just perfect. I return to my eyebrows and am liking the angled brush; I am quite adept at doing my eyebrows, since the coffee table incident and within minutes they are perfect. I then blend some darker eyeshadow along the eye liner, giving my eyes a smoky, sultrier look.

My eyelashes are very short and require that I use a 3 in one mascara for maximum effect; it adds a touch of drama and ensures my eyes stand out. Plus, I need something to stick the false ones to. I return to the highlighter adding just a touch to the end of my nose and blending it slightly for a cute but still natural effect.

I trace the lip pencil around my lips, pouting them slightly. I cannot afford lip implants not on a school-teacher's salary, so this is the closest I get to plump, beautiful lips. My lipstick is a far from subtle baby pink, and with just a dash of shimmering highlighter to their centre gives them a bit of additional dimension; it makes them look super sexy too. While the brush is in my hand, I apply a tiny bit of highlighter along my cheekbone.

My face is barely recognisable, and I feel a different person as I weigh up whether to apply false lashes and rhinestones or lip gloss first...such decisions!

The eye lashes win, and I apply them carefully, pinching them to my newly formed natural lashes. A few rhinestones and lashings of sparkly lip gloss later, I'm ready to get dressed.

My dress is a full-length sequin and rhinestone fish tail number. It shines from every angle and I have waited a long time to see the two together, but even now I have a few additional touches before I look in the full-length mirror. Shoes, high silver stiletto's and jewellery; it wouldn't be complete without some extra sparkle. Not real diamonds, not even real zirconia, just paste or glass but none the less they look the part. Finally, my wig. I had considered getting my hair done, as it had been a bit of a palaver trying to get my hair underneath the condom cap, but for an arm and a leg I could buy a decent sparkly pink wig that matched my dress perfectly. And I couldn't have gone into school Monday morning with pink sparkly hair, so the wig it was. I am, forced to look in the mirror in order to put it on though; I fix my gaze on the wig, trying to keep myself from seeing the whole ensemble.

Finally, the wig is on and I turn away from the mirror, slowly taking a few steps before turning around with my eyes closed. I feel my heart racing with excitement, and I hope I'm not sweating too much. I open my eyes as slowly as possible, every inch of my body trembling with excitement. I almost want to cry tears of joy as I look at the glamourous and very beautiful woman in the mirror. There is no trace of year 2 SATS, Dan, late night marking or drab ill-fitting clothes. I am gorgeous, beyond words!

My phone rings to tell me my taxi has arrived. I had booked it as soon as I had known about tonight. That had been the easy part it was the rest of the getting ready that had taken real thought and careful planning. It is only a fifteen-minute drive to the venue, but right now it feels like forever. I can see the venue, an old cinema converted into a nightclub and I can feel my stomach churn slightly.

There are so many thoughts racing through my mind.

"Can I really do this? Jeez, Dan has a lot to answer for… what am I thinking? I couldn't just get a haircut or tattoo like everyone else after a break-up…Oh no!"

'That'll be twelve quid please love…'

'Oh yes of course…sorry I was miles away.' As I scrabble around in the little clutch that came with the dress, my thoughts are becoming more and more blurry.

'Here you go…keep the change.'

'Thanks love.'

"Ok deep breaths…deep breaths…think calm thoughts…and breathe."

I must be nervous as I've already reached the door without noticing.

The man on the entrance is looking at me and I get the feeling I may have been stood there looking dumbfounded for a while.

'Hey there girl what number are you,' he says gesturing to his list.

'Oh… Er contestant number 5'.

'Well, you look stunning so in you go…that way,' he points his pen in the direction of the door marked backstage '… and break a leg honey.'

I've been on stage and sang plenty of times before, I was a

31

singer long before I was a teacher, but this is a national competition so I'm up against the best there is.

In my head I can hear me telling myself, 'Just stay calm... Deep breath, inhale and exhale...stay calm...no! Calm... Deep breath, deep breath, deep breath... Oh just get your shit together girl!'

I can feel the stagehand touching my arm "You're up next sugar...knock `em dead!" I feel slightly reassured and a little bit side-tracked by how cute the stagehand is, but I don't have time right now, I can hear the hostess of the show introducing me. The same big build up that all of us get.

'Please welcome contestant number 5... She is not the Duchess, not the Princess, not even the Queen... Why no!' She shakes her head, wagging her finger emphatically at the audience all the while building the tension to a crescendo.

'Why no!' she emphasizes further... 'She is...of course...the Empress!'

And this is it, my moment of glory, my chance to be this year's "Drag Idol."

IV THE EMPEROR

THE EMPEROR
To Know, To Will, To Share the Joke
Diane Narraway

"There's a new Flash Gordon film on at the cinema any chance we can go?" Callum piped up, his eyes shining under the mop of ginger hair.

"I don't see why not...we could go this weekend if you like," his mother rarely denied her younger son anything.

This was a typical scene in the Hilton household. Mark and his live-in girlfriend perched on the sofa with his younger brother cross legged on the floor in front of them while the boys' parents occupied the two armchairs.

They were a quirky household to say the least. Mark, resident dropout was a lot like his father but without the belly...or income, for that matter.

The father was intelligent, well respected in his field; lecturing advanced maths at one of the city's more prestigious colleges and designing helicopters for the Navy. It was safe to say that Roy Hilton was the ruler of the house.

It would be an accurate assessment of his household to say that neither the house nor his lifestyle ever reflected his income. It was equally safe to say his family didn't either! Roy was a product of his time. He drank more than he should, and his sense of humour was as dark as his thinning hair; becoming bawdier with each drink.

Yet, for all that he recognised his elder son as 'a chip off the old block' albeit a more anarchic, and on the whole, more sober chip. Mark was the rebel of the family; all long hair and loud rock music, his girlfriend likewise. Mark's father always joked but was slightly in awe of the fact that his son had gone away for the weekend and where normal kids would've brought home a stick of rock, he had brought home a girlfriend.

The girlfriend too had that rebel streak, but she was compassionate and often helped Callum with his schoolwork; he was dyslexic, emotionally immature and struggled in all the subjects and aspects of life his elder brother had excelled at. Also, Callum was tall and with an unruly mop of ginger hair while Mark was shorter with long almost black hair. They couldn't have been more different, and Mark and his friends often joked that Callum was the milkman's! All three of them Roy, Mark and the girlfriend shared the same sense of humour which was beyond Callum and bizarrely beyond his mother too.

The Girlfriend peered over Callum's shoulder too see what the dates for the film were, as she was considering taking him if his mother was busy; she liked Callum and she had enjoyed 'The Wrath of Khan' well enough. Her eyes widened and she nudged Mark, gesturing with her head towards the cinema advert.

Mark bit his lip, desperately trying to stifle the laugh and tirade of comments that were bubbling just below the surface. The girlfriend, likewise, her eyes conveying to Mark how delicious it might be to say nothing. It was hard to decide which would be the most satisfying and hilarious outcome; mentioning it now or letting them find out for themselves.

Truth to tell, there was little love lost between the mother and the girlfriend. However, the giggle became impossible to stifle as the potential scenarios played out in both Mark and the girlfriends' imaginations.

At this point the father, who until now had occupied 'his' armchair in the corner like an Empiric Buddha peered questioningly up from his paper, while the mother threw disapproving glances towards them, suspecting she was the butt of the joke, as only a few days earlier the girlfriend had said how she thought it was nice that they put subtitles on the TV to help the blind; and she had fallen for it hook, line and sinker much to her embarrassment.

Within minutes all eyes were on Mark and his girlfriend, all of which were demanding to know the joke.

Wiping the tears of laughter from her face the girlfriend eventually managed a sort of breathless squeaking. "It's not Flash Gordon…it's Flesh Gordon!"

V THE HIEROPHANT

THE HIEROPHANT
An Ancient Rite - Diane Narraway

Black portentous clouds fill the skies,
With howling winds that shake the dead:
Thunderous roars and lightning flashes
Filling many a wearied soul with dread.

This night I'll stand beneath the chaos,
Oppressive, thick and dark,
That weighs so heavy on my mind
And heavier still within my heart.

For age has been the cruellest master
For far too many days and nights;
My mind growing ever weaker
As my hair is turned to white.

But here within these sacred stones,
The wisdom of my many years
Shall be coupled with a strength of mind
As the storm above rages fierce.

A pinch of cobweb gathered
On the summer solstice morn,
Spun by the venomous widow
In the twilight of the dawn.

Rose petals collected by a lover,
Although she was taken from me
By the icy cold hand of death;
I pray her spirit now is free

Some beeswax fit for a queen
Tempered with some honey,
Mixed with the ashes of
A hanged man's spirit money.

Just a drop of fresh morning dew
With some nettles that don't sting:
A tinge of blue taken from
A raven's severed wing.

And on a glorious midsummer
I caught the rays from the burning sun:
Blended with the pious heart
Of a Puritanical nun.

Add the rattle of a serpent,
And to a powder they are ground
With just a drop of my own blood,
The ingredients are bound.

In candlelight I call to thee,
Gods and spirits of this land:
To the mighty legions of hell
And to the souls of the damned.

I seek my youthful mind:
My cunning and profundity,
My sharp quick wittedness,
And my demonic subtlety.

By all the power of Lucifer,
And all the rulers of the East,
I invoke the powers of insight
And the clarity of the beast.

By all dark powers of Satan,
And all the rulers of the South,
I invoke the power of the adversary
My words seeking to provoke.

By all the powers of Leviathan,
And the rulers of the West,
I invoke the power of the serpent
With its keen intelligence.

By all the powers of Belial,
And all the rulers of the North,
To be master of my thought
And intellect I call thee forth.

Hekate of the crossroads,
I ask for wisdom to know the way,
That my inner sight be
As clear as the light of day.

Let me see far beyond,
The horizon of the mind,
To all that lies unknown
To the spiritually blind.

My hair can stay as white as white,
Pure as the morning driven snow,
But my mind must remain as sharp
As the blade of a pirate cutthroat.

Spirits of this realm, heed my words
Amidst the chaos of this night.
My words have the power of all time,
Bring me the gift of inner sight.

Furies cry and harpies call
And storm rage through this land,
Deliver to me all I ask of thee
For as my will is my command.

VI THE LOVERS

THE LOVERS
A Card Trick Gone Wrong - Defoe Smith

Our world spins along with a massive collection of other objects, all coming along for the ride. A card tumbles as it flicks from the deck. The other card players have seen the card's markings but now they bet on which way up it will land...Face up? Face down? Forward or reversed?

The Queen of Hearts bounces on her corner before flipping face down, and then the suspense; the delicate touch of the dealer's hand teasing the edge of the card as his eyes make contact with each person at the table, inside he is secretly willing that her heart isn't irreparably broken.

The dealer flicks at the edge of the card as if it were a tiddly wink, and as the card turns, tiny beads of blood string off, powered by momentum leaving tiny splatters on the green felt...that's life, and all the while, our world continues to turn, along with the mass of other objects in the universe.

The Queen of Hearts is done for, she's imprisoned. Beaten with a *Club* and trapped in this set of cards...tricked! And now, after all she has been through, after the years of servitude human-un-kind her royal highness is sent on a cyclonic journey through the air. Her card is marked. Her royal blood is spilt and when it comes to the balance of love and hate, dark and light, the players hands are awash with as much blood, as the same person who gave her blessings in matters of the heart.

Sometime, before all this, life was grand! She once stood tall, the sixth in her house and one of the boldest. Making life choices in court for her subjects was no lightly undertaken matter and never did she think so. Loves choices and opportunities traditionally, could only be undertaken by members of the court...specifically, The House of Hearts.

43

As the name suggests, The House of Hearts is responsible for all matters of the heart, it could mend a heart and it could break it. Through thousands and thousands of years, since the beginning of feelings this has been the way, and this is how it should've remained.

The one rule that was paramount above all others for the House of Hearts was that they must never proclaim the gift of love as their own, and therein lay the problem; the Queen had been royally caught with her pants down, literally, in a full passionate embrace with a right diamond geezer…a Prince, as it happened.

Never, in a very long time had such a tragedy come to light and knowing what the punishment for such a serious crime was; the Queen had to be under some spell, or even suffering the effects of lunacy to even think that she would be able to have her cards and shuffle them!

They say love is blind, regardless of the risks or the hurt caused. In that one moment, all that matters, is the rush of warmth that is washed in positive emotion; the heightened taste of the forbidden fruit of the sin tree, and the rush of getting away with it!

The House of Hearts was taught the ancient scriptures from a very early age;
"Love is not blind. Love is cold and calculated, carefully planned to ensure maximum productivity and longevity." Over time the Queen obviously discovered the hard way, that accidents happen and the rule of free will is as heavily embedded into the very fibre of society, just as much as the rules and regulations of 'tradition.'

Whilst sat in her cell, the Queen of Hearts had time to cast her mind back to the events that led to her slipping from grace. From the corner of her dark and damp cell with its persistent drip from the ceiling that led to a carefully placed bowl on the floor. Each drip echoed another memory that flashed in her mind; faces, places, actions, feelings, love, hate, passion, compassion… Pain!

Finally, her mind settles on the moment her lover first approached her and his attempts to gain her favour.

At first, the memories seemed clouded and partial, skipping twixt the first moment when her 'Prince Oh So Charming' caught her gaze, to the moment she first fell under his spell. The words he muttered, the delicate kiss to her neck and then the gentle touch of his soft and slightly trembling hand as it moved slowly down her body from her neck to her breast.

Yep it sounds cliché, and it is very much so and that was the purpose of this particular 'tempter.'

"Love is not blind. Love is cold and calculated, carefully planned to ensure maximum productivity and longevity."

"Drip, drip, drip..." Suddenly it all clicked, and she quickly fell into a reminiscent daze. It now became apparent. Wide-eyed, enraged, and ravished in more ways than one, she realised she had been betrayed! Not just by the one who she thought her lover, but also by her own emotions...but why?

Society was good, everything was exactly as it should be. To tip the balance of things, to remove that structure which the very foundations of their world was based upon, *that* would be nothing less than treason in the eyes of the court.

The Queen on the other hand, took it straight to the heart. Always in a position of servitude, never feeling the rampant excited heartbeat of arousal or the confused thoughts of the mind...only duty...until now!

She remembered many, many, moons ago, a case of two young hearts beating to the same rhythm. Recalling how, as she looked into their tear-soaked eyes, clear evidence that they had both stared at the same stars was apparent. Emotion ruled their moment and that alone was grounds for ruling in favour of the court...banishment to the deck for the girl and the young lad was to be recycled into society and allotted a position into the house of diamonds...case closed! (For now).

As the young lad climbed the ranks of the House of Diamonds, he never once stopped thinking about his lost love. Over time he had somehow managed to temper himself to show no emotion or signs of the heartbreak he had suffered, instead he secretly hatched a plan, one that would undoubtably break the foundations of the courts! He would exact his revenge upon the very person who had stolen the love of his life.

The Queen of Hearts *would* feel the raw pain of having her own emotions torn away, just as he and his lover had. She would be drugged and stripped of all that gave her such a high status. Then she too would spend the last of her days trapped and voiceless! She would be cast out and played over and over again, becoming a part of her own creation...the deck!

It was thought, that the deck held a portal to the land's only prison, nobody had ever returned from there! This, however, was hearsay...scary stories that were rumoured throughout society and passed down through generations that told of the place where 'free thinkers' and 'naughty tinkers' were sent. Over time this had become the most-told scary bed-time story that parents told to their young, much like our tales of 'The Bogeyman' or 'Peter Geeky.' Obviously, those that ruled were privy to the facts, but to speak of those facts meant banishment to the deck.

Every experience forms and shapes who we are, and the Queen was no exception, dealing with matters of the House on a daily basis, where every possible scenario and outcome had to be considered. This in itself, would make the strongest willed of people shake, yet she was expected to stand tall and not buckle under the wonderment of desire, the shimmering enticement of free will. But now all that she ever knew is now gone.

Our world spins along with a massive collection of other objects coming along for the ride, the card tumbles as it is flicked from the deck.

The other prison guards who are playing glance up at the dealer as they have seen the cards markings and realise its past importance. The dealer is smiling, he thought all bets were off…but how wrong he was! They are betting on which way up it lands. Face up? Face down? Forward or reversed?

The Queen of Hearts bounces on her corner, before flipping face down smashing her nose against the face of the card…and then comes the suspense! The delicate touch of the dealer's hand teasing the edge of the card, as his eyes make contact with each person around the table. Inside he is secretly willing that her heart isn't irreparably that her heart isn't irreparably broken…he needs this card more than he needs the air he breathes.

The dealer flicks at the edge of the card as if it were a tiddly wink and as the card turns, tiny beads of blood string off, powered by momentum, leaving tiny splatters on the green felt. She closes her eyes, sighs and takes her last breath as her heart shatters into a million pieces. That's life! Our world still turns along with a mass of other objects in the universe.

And what of the Prince of Diamonds? He never got the satisfaction of the revenge he so eagerly sought. When his long-lost lover never returned; he watched the Queen's demise; exemplifying just how cruel he had become. Dealing the deck out to his fellow guardsmen served only as a reminder that - for every action there is indeed a reaction!

VII THE CHARIOT

THE CHARIOT
Alternative routes - Defoe Smith

A friend once said it is all a test, just make the most of what you
do as we are all a long time dead.
Take one sip from the cosmic grail
but do not worry, you won't get off your head.

The upsides generally come with a downside though.
Mine is late night self-doubt.
That is when the bully in me comes out and that is totally fine;
at least no one else sees the side of me that's an asshole.

The melt down moments, looking back are the ones that make
me smile the most.
The memories still so vivid, even the emotions come back,
coupled with the rare moments where the upper hand can be
gained.
I merely share to relate and not to boast.

It happens to us all at some point or another.
It happened to me just the other day.
There I was re-reading a poem I had wrote, when the all familiar
negativity crept in like a conniving little scrote.

The grammar is wrong in the sentence.
The deadline is way, way, over-due!
Singulars or plurals!
Awkward bloody sentences.
One lump or two? "Begone foul demons!" I inwardly
proclaimed.
"Leave the devil to his bloat!"

Then I hit the select all, followed by delete and beat myself at my
own game,
whilst the devil in me, sat the fuck down and rewrote.

My bully, self-confidence crumbled
with each refined and sharpened word, flowing through chapter
by chapter,
scrawling through rambling notes;
the pain of my self-doubt dying, could be heard.

I re-read the rewriting and weep,
and when came the morning
(3 am) like any other there was no inner voice.
I had fed off the victor,
and now with thumb and forefinger
I aim for the burning wick and smother.

The sound of the morning chorus blasts a tuneful cough,
reminding me of the time I woke up in grandpa's aviary...
Black birds, Tits, Dunnocks and Robins,
all had their say, well, some just perched on the fence
Looking down at me in the planter trough.
I often sleep out under the stars.

It brings forth a sense of calm.
Sometimes it's easy to assume weakness will win, when really,
we are strong as the universe,
or at least an old American car.

So, the chariot's been carting my ass for far too long.
It's time to let the horses rest
and throw the bags up on my back.
The balance is not meant to sit central.
It isn't meant to be on track.

VIII JUSTICE

JUSTICE
Frenching the Bully - Lou Hotchkiss Knives

Write hard and clear about what hurts.
Ernest Hemingway.

The automated doors before me slide open with swift, mechanical deference, and I enter. At last.

Here I am, perched on my highest Westwood heels, power dressed to fuck: designer coat, hat, gloves, pencil skirt. A second ago I checked my face in my pocket mirror to ensure the make-up is on solid and that I look like a car-stopping Botticelli virgin.

Except I'm no virgin. Not anymore.

My heart is pounding.

In front of me stretches the eighth circle of hell - a pandemonium of ironmongery with its seemingly never ending aisles of metal and plastic goods, tools, screws of various sizes and shapes, plugs and knobs, garden furniture, pots, taps, lamps, bath tubs and toilet seats; you name it. Not the kind of place Wordsworth would visit in order to wander lonely as a cloud. The store is heaving with customers - crafty housewives dragging their moaning brood in their sillage, beer-bellied DIY enthusiasts, clueless students in search of the best bookshelf or bedsit lighting. Amidst the crowd, a handful of overworked shop assistants dressed in prison-orange buzz around like panicked bees.

I feel absolutely incongruous in the midst of all this agitation and brouhaha. But it doesn't matter. I'm not here because I want to decorate my flat.

I'm here to find you.

It's been fifteen years. It was only last night that I was screaming it from the stage, spitting into the microphone, my knuckles white with fury. I am a punk singer, one who doesn't pull punches.

It's been fifteen years of self-loathing
But I know, I know where you live.

Fifteen years of nightmares, flashbacks, anxiety, early morning sobs, afternoons wasted reliving time after time the same scenarios, your words still echoing in my head.

You worthless cunt... Why don't you go kill yourself...?
You are a waste of life... Freak... You fucking freak... Shut up or I'll hit you again... Lower your gaze... I said lower your gaze!

I'm twenty-eight and I've never seen fire. I'm neither a soldier nor a terror victim. Yet I carry the weight of what you've put me through like a 30 kilos rucksack full of explosives and dirty, bloodied bandages. Apparently, it's PTSD.

For a split second I wonder if you'll recognise me. What if you have forgotten me? Maybe you're the kind of psychopath who can shove any less-than-glorious memory in a corner of your brain like it's a bag of dirty laundry you don't want to deal with, and then carry on with your life as if nothing ever happened. If that's the case, I certainly envy you. I remember everything.

It was 1991 and the grimy grunge years were in full swing. I was thirteen, and you'd just turned fifteen. I was four foot five, scrawny, spotty, still pre-pubescent. But you...you looked like a dream.

I remember the first time I saw you undress, in the PE changing rooms. You were tall and blonde and built like the porn version of a pre-Raphaelite water nymph. I had stopped right in my tracks the second you took off your shirt, fascinated by the vision of your glorious, brand new femininity. You stood in the midst of our vulgar, acneic, Impulse-scented crowd like Aphrodite emerging from the sea on a Cyprus beach. A swan amongst battery chickens. I remember thinking I'd never seen someone as beautiful as you in real life, only ever on television.

53

As I stood in my little girl's underwear, utterly transfixed, you suddenly noticed my awe-struck gaze. And Holy Moly, you didn't like it one bit. This was the moment when everything changed.

You threw yourself at me, sending me flying to the floor, screaming abuse as you pulled my hair tight in your fist.

Look at me like that again and I'll knock your lights out, you screamed, turning instantly and terrifyingly from Angel to Banshee.

You little piece of shit...you ugly little piece of shit.

I was so terrified I couldn't utter a word. You shoved me against the wall with a snort before, casually, launching into a conversation with one of your cronies, leaving me shaken and subdued, fighting back the tears. I hadn't meant any harm. *I just thought you were beautiful.*

Whatever you saw as the nature of my crime, you condemned me, that day, to a very long sentence. For two and a half years you didn't give me a day's rest, taunting me, following me around with your mob of loud, vulgar, creepy admirers, all of them all too happy to gang up on an easy target in the hope of obtaining your favours. What wouldn't they have done for you, the Alpha female, the bad-ass calendar blonde, the wild girl who intimidated even the school staff? So, they fought your war, egging each other on to see which dog would be the most loyal, which wolf could bite the hardest. This is what emotionally crippled teenage boys do when they want pussy. My first name was dropped altogether. To everyone, I became "Ugly," some kind of Quasimodo figure, at best a verbal target, at worst a dehumanised punching ball. My life became a long litany of public humiliations and physical abuse, and here I am, fifteen years later, still haunted by the memory of every incident. The obscene graffiti. The stolen schoolbags, the defaced homework. The rape threats. The mocking chants. The blows.

Damn. I shouldn't have started that vicious cycle of reminiscing again. I can feel my breath getting shallow, my body tensing into fight or flight mode. There is an iron-wrought bench in a corner of the garden section; Faux-Edwardian, priced at 199 pounds. I decide to sit down for a few minutes and try to calm down.

It's not easy, knowing that you are here, somewhere in this building, hiding like a Minotaur in this unlikely neon-lit labyrinth.

What am I going to find, when I finally pluck the courage to face you? From a friend, I have heard that you are married with children. I wince at the thought. Are people like you really capable of love, or is it all an act? Can someone who attempted to throw another child from a second-floor window be a good mother? What kind of moral guide are you, when you got a gang of boys to strip me to my underwear and dump me in a bin, whilst the whole class watched and cheered like a mob of bystanders at a witch trial?

It took years for the pain to finally turn to rage. Only then did I realise the extent of my hatred for you. I have hated you more than life itself. I have hated you to distraction, to exhaustion. You have no idea what I have fantasised about doing to you. In my daydreams, I would torture you for hours. I would spit at you, square in the face, exactly like you spat at me day after day, big, greasy, yellow, bacteria-oozing gobs. I would break your every bone with all the refinement of an aspiring Torquemada in petticoats. Do you know how horrific it is, to realise that you, who were once the victim, are now capable of entertaining such thoughts? I never used to be this monster. You taught me well.

For years I have begged the heavens for justice, for revenge; for you to receive the just wage of your sins. In the confines of my room, I would elaborate wild plans to turn up on your doorstep with a loaded rifle and make you confess and beg for forgiveness in front of your nearest and dearest. Or, more deviously, I would fantasise about leading your husband astray and destroying your marriage. *Who cares what he actually looks like?* I would repeat to myself, drunk on wrath and injustice. *I've been so fucked I can take any dick.* At the time, I would have done anything to make you pay, regardless of the manner employed. No blow would have been too low if it meant you suffered.

A vague pain interrupts my train of thoughts. In spite of the thickness of my coat, that overpriced iron-wrought bench is now digging into my buttocks and it hurts. I get up and continue wandering through the tortuous paths of the DIY Erebus you call your place of work.

Around my twenty-sixth birthday, something changed. It suddenly dawned on me that, by spending my days wallowing in anger and resentment, I was allowing you, somehow, to continue hurting me. Exhausted as I was, and by now determined never to let you hurt me again, I decided to finally concentrate on my well-being instead of wasting my youth on fruitless fantasies of vengeance. Letting go of you turned out to be a mammoth task - how do you fall out of hate with someone you've been obsessing over for more ten years? Not to mention the obvious - how do you learn self-acceptance, when you have become addicted to self-harm? How do you form lasting relationships, when you are convinced, deep down, that you are unlovable? Every day, of the past two years has been an experiment in rebirth and self-creation. How do you find yourself when you've been lost for so long? How do you extract yourself from the well of loneliness, and what do you do when you finally emerge?

It took a lot of efforts, and many setbacks, to finally settle into some kind of normality. Even now, as I purposely procrastinate, pretending to peruse through displays of brightly coloured pots of paint, I feel the grip of doubt close around my insides, and my resolve is faltering. Only a few hours ago, in my room, when I was applying layer upon layer of make-up in attempt to conceal from you my bruised, fucked-up soul, I was convinced seeing you again would bring me some kind of closure. Now I'm not so sure. What am I hoping to get from this encounter? What are the most likely scenarios to unfold when we finally come face to face? All too often, in life, we find ourselves weak in the face of opportunity. Nothing could happen. We may just acknowledge each other and exchange platitudes, unable to face or discuss our common past for the weight of its implications, cowardly burying our heads in the sand as our fifteen-year old elephant destroys everything in the room.

What good could come out of such an encounter?

There must be another alternative, I tell myself aloud, still pretending to read the composition label of a pot of Deluxe Valentine. *Gods, you're speaking aloud again. Freak.*

Allowing the devil on my shoulder to take temporary hold on my imagination, I suddenly picture myself launching at you in slow motion, claws out and wailing like a harpy, with Drowning Pool's *Bodies* playing at intolerable levels in the background. Although the whole scene has a satisfying Tarantino-like aesthetic about it, it certainly doesn't pass the reality test, even for a minute. For a start, I don't have the required degree of psychopathy to gouge your eyes out. And even if I managed to deliver a few meaningful punches, security would undoubtedly arrive within minutes, putting an end to what would turn out to be, with hindsight, a crushingly embarrassing scene. I would most likely end up with a criminal record and a hefty fine to pay. All that for what? I would end up the villain, and you the victim. Where's the Justice in that?

I notice I have started pacing the aisle to and fro, the pot of vermillion paint still in my hand. *Try to look natural.* Nonchalantly, I grab a pot of ultramarine blue. *Keep your head down.*

What, indeed, is Justice? Fair retribution, levelling, compensation? Is Justice the produce of a system of values inherited from fair, unbiased Gods, or is it just another flawed, fleeting human ideal? Does Justice serve vengeance, or is vengeance only a filthy by-product of Justice? Can Justice ever deliver true peace of mind?...

Standing here, dolled-up as for a rendezvous, yet tense and combat-ready, am I seeking revenge, I wonder, or adjustment? What do I want, exactly? Who is that person I am longing to meet at the dawning of that fifteen-years postponed duel? Someone to crush? Somebody, perhaps, whose recent misfortunes would right my wrongs?

Wouldn't it be wonderful if you were now fat, ugly, and as powerless as I once was... Am I seeking someone I could suddenly, finally feel superior to, someone in whose face I could raise a perfectly manicured middle-finger whilst cooing '*where is your God now, bitch*?' ... Somehow, it doesn't feel right.

A dull nausea overcomes me. Truth be told, I don't see the point in descending to your level, of becoming the bully I so utterly loathe. For years I have hated you with a passion, yet I have, of late, grown tired of hatred, and these days, I'd rather be the bigger person. Still, I am acutely aware that seeing you again might trigger me into acting like an arsehole. The temptation is there.

At that moment, a song comes up on the shop's sound system, a song I know; I just cannot remember the name of the artist.

'I'm sitting down here but hey you can't see me...'

I put the pots of paint down, turn around, look up right in front of me, and gasp.

That blonde woman, sitting at a desk at the end of the aisle, in the kitchen section, is you, unmistakably. I would recognise that blunt fringe, those curls anywhere. My vision becomes blurred. I notice my pulse accelerating as I stride in your direction, as if moved by an invisible, irrepressible force. I am not thinking, I am just walking; I can hear every clatter of my heels on the linoleum floor. Here you are.

'Hello,' I blurt out.

You raise your head from the paperwork you were in the process of examining, and all of a sudden, all the tension leaves my body as if by magic. The old veneer has cracked. I had somehow expected to find before me the teenage nymph of yore, she who was so tall, so lean, so utterly terrifying; yet fifteen years have passed, and there is nothing remotely scary left about you. Gone is the bold, ruby-red lipstick, the heavy eyeliner, the evil glint in your eye. You look somewhat heavier - don't we all - squat and tired-looking; your clothes have seen better days, and only the bright orange, mandatory badge of the shop employees distinguishes you from the multitude. You could be anyone and everyone. At that moment, the image of you I had built and held in my mind for so long - that of the demonic, vicious schoolyard harpy - completely vanishes. *You are...normal.*

"Can I help you?" you ask in the neutral tone salespeople automatically adopt when they're on their twentieth customer of the day. Your face is open and politely inquisitive.

You don't know who I am.

I feel my cheeks turn hot and cherry-red. Hopefully my full-coverage foundation will adequately conceal the worst of the flush. A thick, surreal silence fills the space between us.

'I would like a kitchen catalogue' I hear myself reply, somewhat dreamily. No sooner have I finished my sentence than a strange boldness grabs hold of me, and the words I was afraid of uttering all along come tumbling out of my mouth.

'You don't remember me, do you?'

Another pause. I feel your eyes scrutinising my face in vain.

'No,' you answer with a blank stare. *Ok. This is now or never.*

'We went to school together. I am Julia. Julia Hepburn.'
Your face drops. *Bingo! You know. You fucking know!*

'My god, I would never have recognised you...!' You
exclaim, laughing nervously, as if trying to brighten the
atmosphere. Do you think I'm being fooled? That smile is
forced, I can see it. You know what's coming. Like two cowboys
at opposites angles of a corral, we nod at each other, unsure of
our next move. Yet I am standing above you and I can feel you
cowering, suddenly vulnerable, hunched over your computer
keyboard, trapped behind your desk like a goldfish in a bowl. So,
I strike. Politely.

'We didn't have the best of times, you and I, back in the
day' I remark in my calmest voice, allowing the end of my
sentence to dangle in the subsequent silence like a subtle threat.

Now you are scared. I keep staring. *I want answers.*

Your face has turned pale, like that of a thief caught in the
act. Tense and fidgeting, you mumble a few tentative sentences,
before finally finding your words, words I had, to be honest,
never expected to hear.

'I am sorry,' you finally exhale, with an air of contrition so
sincere it stops me right in my tracks.

'So sorry. At the time, it was...I am not trying to justify
what I did, but...that time, when we were at school, was an
incredibly dark period of my life.'

Fuck you!

'It was very hard for me, too' I shoot back instantly, as
stern as a judge and towering just as straight. 'Do you remember
how it started? That day in the changing room? I just wanted to
like you, to be your friend. Why on earth did you have to do this
shit?! Why?!'

Immediately I bite my lips, realising I've gone too far.
This is too personal a conversation to have at your work desk at
four o'clock on a Saturday afternoon. What do you remember,

60

anyway? People like you have selective memory. Every villain is a hero in their own narrative.

Your jawline is droopy. There's something bovine and gormless about you these days, but I can't bring myself to rejoice in the contemplation of it.

So, bitch, what's your excuse?...

'Sometimes things happen to girls...things that really, really mess them up' you reply in a low, broken voice.

Silence. You hold my gaze intently, as if I should know. *Should know what?...*

Suddenly the penny drops, and I understand.

I understand because I, too, have been raped. But I could never tell you, not now, not here, not after all we've been through. Long suppressed images flash before my eyes as I am overcome by a maelstrom of memories. I see that beautiful boy with cornflower-blue eyes, that very boy who betrayed me in the worst possible way, and defiled love by turning what should have been a night of cuddles and pleasure into a purgatory of sorrow and suffering.

As relentless as crashing waves, my recollections knock me off balance, threatening to submerge me under the weight of a myriad of unleashed emotions: the shock of the assault, the unparalleled agony of his dick stabbing through my insides, so real the mere evocation of it is enough for my body to almost go into shock. The long minutes I spent breathless, folded in two, limp from the hurt, my cervix bruised and bleeding - I relive it all.

There's a lump in my throat as big as a walnut. It chokes and hurts, and I cannot utter a word. So, I stare at you, my vision blurred by hot, bitter tears that drown everything into a tunnel of barely - contained emotions. It all makes sense now. That day, in the changing rooms, what you thought you saw when I was gazing at you was enough to trigger you into an outburst of violence that, somehow, made you feel back in control when you

61

unleashed it upon me. I know only too well what that bottled up fury can do. I've lived with it for almost a decade. Yet, for all the compassion I feel for you in this moment, I cannot forget that you took it out on me...*on me*, you fucking cunt! And by doing so you took away fifteen years of my life.

If only I could tell you this.

I just can't speak.

Do you know that I know? We stare at each other in silence, our eyes screaming while our lips remain sealed. I could swear you too are fighting back the tears.

'I'm sorry' you say again. 'So sorry.' Now your voice is truly breaking. You hold out your hand and, without thinking, I take it in mine. How surreal, to hold your hand and know that it is that very same hand that hit me day after day for two years; yet there is no animosity, no weariness in your touch, just a quiet acknowledgment of our shared suffering.

'You really fucked me up.'

'I know.'

'Do you have children...?'

'I have five....'

Your grip on my hand tightens. '...And I don't want them to go through any of *that.*'

Whatever that last sentence means, I cannot but agree. Talking with you is an exercise in paraphrase and innuendo. We will never be able to name the "unnameable," we can only tiptoe around volcanoes of meaning.

'No one should ever have to go through it.'

'I know. I wish I could turn back time.'

Where do we go from here? There is only one way out, so I take it. The time has come to put the demons to sleep.

'I forgive you,' I say, finally allowing the tears to flow. It is your turn to cry.

'Thank you, thank you' you repeat. 'Thank you.'

62

I am glad there's no one else queuing at your desk, because we both look like hell with our mascara running down our cheeks. After a few minutes we manage to collect ourselves and let out a sigh.

There are many things I would like to tell you, now that we have come to a place of understanding; but I am well aware that our brand-new empathy doesn't extend into the realm of complete sentences.

'I wish you to be happy, and your children too.'

'I wish you to be happy too. You deserve it, after all I've put you through.'

'I can't forget what happened, but I am happy to forgive. It's time to move on...'

'It is.'

'Thank you for understanding. Goodbye, for now.'

'Goodbye' you say.

I turn around. Through the automated doors in the distance, the daylight looks like a tunnel of white and distant sky blue.

Another song comes on the sound system, and I can swear, at that moment, that the angels have whacked their favourite playlist on just so I can stride out of your DIY hell looking like a female Dante in high heels, hair flick and all.

'I can see clearly now the rain is gone...'

Is this justice? ... I prefer to think of it as adjustment.

IX THE HERMIT

THE HERMIT
The Way of All Things - Rachael Moss

The solstice sun, a burnished bronze, falls on the horizon scattering glowing embers that flicker on trees standing trembling in a wandering wind. It winds its way, creaking in their stark, bleak, nakedness, their seeds spent and quivering on the rain wetted earth, glinting in the lengthening rays. Sinking lower, deepening into a rich russet that inflames the pelt of a soft-footed fox snaking through the woodland intent on a scent that quickened his nostrils, the sun slips. It spills its light into the twisting, writhing river so that it seethes in gleaming copper, thrashing, hurrying, on its undulating way to return to the great mother, its voice sweet and soothing as it swirls, glancing off rocks, tumbling over tree roots, ever-changing but still remaining the same, delighting in the nature of its longing.

The sun slams down and the wood darkens in a bone-cold chill, the river becomes a black serpent tossing and spitting and the trees wave their blackened branches at the livid sky. A screech pierces through the low rumbling of the waters and hissing of the winds that slap and swipe, hell-bent on their meanderings. Somewhere in the gloom an owl hunts down a creature pinned to the fetid ground in terror…its final shriek unheard in its last moment of life as talons stab its pulpy flesh. Creatures unseen sniff the air at the sudden stench of blood, yearning for its tang upon the tongue.

The darkness deepens with the cold, the floor hardens and contracts, trees loom black and glowering, swaying a macabre dance. The night suffocates, throttling the dusk, and clouds clog up the sky, the moon smothered behind their heavy bulk. But sitting on the muddied riverbank, bare feet ankle deep in the keening waters, she's there, silent and still, alit from a light that seeps through her pores. Skin pale, head tilted towards the flowing waters, her eyes shine a strange light, the air all around her pulsing.

She's felt all this over and over; the stab of excitement and pain when the otter bitch, reeling through the slipstream currents of the murky brook, strikes the trout. The desperate screams of the dog-fox and vixen as they remain stuck together in the final part of their mating ritual, securing the mixing of fluids and cells in the dance of generation. The bee that gathers pollen from a blossom radiant in its wantonness; and the heat from a falling star crashing through space like a flash of understanding in the mind.

Close by, within a nest of crinkly leaves buried a little in the musty earth, a dormouse quietly snores, curled up in its bushy tail, the beat of its heart slow. Below this, but above where the tree roots cleave their way down and through the fermenting soil, an acorn is softening in the damp, gestating.

She sits unmoving, her left hand gripping a gnarly staff, its tip buried in the crystallised mud in the bank. Her seat balanced on the edge, legs plunging downwards into the blackened currents, her right arm stretched forwards, in her hand something shines, sending the dim shadows into light. She's been poised like this since the sun began to set.

Through her life, she's fought the demons that gnaw and claw, the ones that stamped her down with their malaise of inadequacy; she destroyed them in her journeying into the darkness. Removing herself from populations blighted with insecurity, ignorance and greed, lusts that ravage, rape and kill to fill vacuums sundered by the dominance of the fearful and their lies and deceit, where the gods once resided. She wrestled those within the dark crevices of the mind that would show their fangs of fear and shame and tempered with love others that skulk. Everywhere she can, she's searched, finding diamonds among the rancidity that lurks and creeps, forging her way on paths of silver through the battlefield.

Challenged with the ravages of a society that birthed her, tried to devour her in its cogs, basing its values on a worthless grasping for the void of materialism and for a false domination, squashing the life force; she sees brilliance hidden below the monstrous beasts of despair and doubt, and the shackles of conformity.

Back then the world of mankind had robbed her of life's intensity, and filled it with rules and meaningless years spent in the pursuit of money, so that she could live asphyxiated in four walls that shut out the singing of the wind and rain, voices of the birds, the heat of golden sunshine, and the touch of the cool moon at midnight. Misery clamped down and tightened its grip. She sensed that the unfurling of a blossom in spring, the careering of the hare in its speedy dance, and the voice of the sea as it breathes restlessly sighing at the shore, had all lost their magick. For many human hearts who were taught to no longer feel, and instead obey, toil, in a vacuous grasping.

But her heart felt. It felt the unbearable pain of the forests as each mighty tree was felled for yet more greed, leaving desolate wastes where no creature could dwell. The terrible despair of those who suffered for their race, sex, or beliefs, it felt the heaviness of a world that had sunken into an ugly, empty, pit.

Skin warmed by the sun, she would hear the flute of Pan wafting through the perfumed meadows in May, under the skylark's song, as the flowers peeled open. Aching, flighted creatures flitting and cavorting all around, and her whole being would stir in immense yearning for something beautifully strange, that was there, always there, glimpsing it, fleetingly, and feel its curious fire raging.

Her heart felt the beauty of world in the iridescence of a starling feather and the breath-taking wonderment of their winter mumurations; the sweet caress of another, naked flesh thrilling in response, and in each person a deep solitude.

She saw death, and death was nothing but a coming into fruition of the seed that germinated, grew, bloomed seeded, germinated...and she saw Love.

But these things were merely just flickers, the essence lay beyond.

Retreating within, she would go to terrifying places, with always the thought of ending her life as she drowned in hopelessness at the brutal shallowness of the world. She would sit for long hours on the woodland's edge under dripping trees, watching lone spiders intricately weave their silken threads between swaying branches, glistening in the setting sun. She would feel for humanity in its fragile transience interconnected with the surging vitality that forms the world and desensitised to the majesty of being burning within each individual. If only they were free to see themselves.

Sometimes she would hear a quiet voice urging her to find the way, and she would have dreams and visions where, on flighty feet, she would storm through brooding darkness, where the origins of all things simmered, seeing her way in the gloom perfectly, and she felt she could help those lost in the bleakness.

Eventually, she was able to steer these visions. She would rampage through the terrible caverns full of horror, and diving down, she would bring back a blazing incandescence that would light her from within. She would see the world from all perspectives; the serpent about to strike, a rat frozen in terror, a chick hatching from its egg into the cold world, sea-creature buried in the deep seabed; the rain as it lashed the stricken valleys. She began to understand the illusion of her aloneness and joy began to slay her anguish.

Dusk would scuttle in, fading garish colours into tapestries of grey, and creatures would rustle in the hedgerows; others, from other realms, would stir in the places between mind and other worlds. Her hands grew hot and restless. When the constellations rampaged the skies, she'd feel them whirling their tales in the vastness inside. Over time, she comprehended and loved the hallowed nature of who she was; not a pawn on a chessboard manipulated by external powers, but an expression whose nature was in manifesting itself freely. The world of humanity was lost within its fear, but she knows the way.

She also knows that fear has a part in a world where all expressions must play themselves out, and every realisation must be fulfilled.

Eventually she came to settle in these woods, drawn by the darkness and deeps that bristled, not seeking light but seeking the murky black where the light can shine the brightest; back to the origins, where primal tentacles dwell and where the springs of love and rapture bubble.

A few tiny fish have collected amongst her toes, squirming, and a badger, foraging away from its subterranean tunnels, white stripes dimly aglow in the night, snuffles for earthworms by her side, in the soil warmed by her heat. An antlered stag disturbs the rhythm of the waters and winds as he suddenly crashes through the trees, snapping twigs, crushing scattered beech masts with his cloven hooves; amber pelt glistening with sweat, his breath steaming and spiralling as it disappears into the freezing gusts. He stops at the riverbank opposite the hermit and lifts his mighty head glancing left and right, the smooth velvet of his tines momentarily silhouetted against the cloud-ridden sky like the twisting branches of the ancient oaks. He lowers his mouth into the water and drinks, gentle lips sucking the cool liquid, quenching his thirst, as it swirls its vortexes, gushing into his warm body that pounds with his heartbeat. Once done, he wades through the river, crossing next to her, sending the scaled bodies of the fish to dart downstream. The badger stumbles off, grunting, silken deer-flank, very slightly, brushing her bare shoulder, fur against flesh, and he continues on his way through the gaps in the whispering trees.

The clouds begin to part and starlight prickles, tingling on the frost-stiffened ground. The wind slows it's song, and the eerily bright coursing hound, Sirius, flickers on the river's quaking surface. The moon flings shrouds from her fuming face and shards of pearl ricochet all around, sparking off trunk and branch, illuminating a startled pigeon that flaps its wings with lightening claps, and shadows weave and meander, throbbing with virile intensity.

The long night spins on, palpitating. The moon sinks and shadows hover, distending and disappearing, and the stars beam brighter. The winds cease their restless prowling, and the fists of Jack Frost grip tighter.

The hermit still sits motionless but she's riding the will of all things, the secrets of life's essence glorifying in its freedom, where all possibilities are potent.

A thin pale light dims the stars and a bleak cry of a crow heralds the twilight. Mercury and Jupiter appear on the horizon, cavorting together, and the solstice morning is birthing. She rises, slowly, deftly, her outline blurred, her form transparent. The forest condensed and lustrous within her shape and permeating out of the edges, expanding; robins with crimson breasts aglow, flitter, tree limbs achingly reach out, uncoiling; it's as if the woods radiate from her. She walks away, away from the day and back into the darkness, disappearing forever into the morning bird cries. Into the buds that lay contracted awaiting the gush of sap to unfurl, the snail hidden under the moist earth, and into the light that glints in the eyes and inflames the heart; to shine the perpetual light of freedom, the way of Love, the way of All things, fertilising the dawn splattered world, as she goes.

X WHEEL OF FORTUNE

WHEEL OF FORTUNE
Red 7 - Diane Narraway

He was tall with beautifully chiselled features, dark eyes which were as black as his hair. He was stunning and would've been hard to miss anywhere, even less so here. She, of course was watching him, not solely for his good looks, but because she was always watching. She didn't miss a trick and she had noticed he was on a winning streak. He was clever about it admittedly; never betting too much and always on a street or a corner but if we had noticed, she was bound to have.

She was tall, blonde, perfectly formed and knew exactly how to play most people to her advantage. Every one of us employees knew their place and woe-betide-you if you crossed her, yet for all that she treated her staff very well. Staff rarely left and as a result, we had become a close-knit community, but more importantly we knew what was expected of us and were damned good at our jobs. I knew that somehow this guy was playing us and if I knew, you could guarantee she knew!

Predictably, it had only ever been a matter of time, before she appeared beside him, carrying two glasses; large bourbon in both. This flustered him slightly, but that seemed to be more about having a beautiful woman come up to him rather than any awareness he had been caught out. She smiled, her perfect smile and he was thrown totally off guard.

"Bourbon? I mean, you look like a bourbon drinker" she held a glass out for him to take.

"Is it Jack Daniels?" He asked attempting to prove some point or other. I don't think he knew exactly why he had asked that as one look at her suggested she was far classier than that.

"Hell no! Its Old Fitzgerald of course!" She swirled the whisky around her glass, sniffing it appreciatively...

"Hard to get hold of, but I keep a bottle for special guests"

He took the other glass from her, sniffed at it and swigged it down in one, truth to tell you could see he, too was just trying to prove a point, but this had reverted into a battle of 'who was, or at least who could appear the coolest'

"Another?" she clicked her fingers for the waiters to bring another.

"I guess so" his feigned nonchalance wasn't really fooling anyone, least of all her.

"I guess, you're wondering why I'm offering you drinks, what do I want in return?"

"Yeah, it's crossed my mind" By this point he was slightly more caught up in her beauty and was positively exuding pheromones - I could even smell the scent of a highly aroused man, so I knew she could. Men! Their dicks nearly always their downfall, and this guy was no exception.

"Well, you're on a winning streak and I like winners" He knew she owned the place and deep down he knew she wasn't gonna like people winning her money, but she was perched on the stool behind him with a dress so low cut it left little to the imagination. And, like I said his brain was being ruled by his cock and so, he was, more or less, happy to buy into anything.

"Say I told you the next number that would come up. No more streets or corners just all in for the big one"

"Sounds wonderful, but I'm not stupid and 2 drinks doesn't make me drunk enough to fall for this"

"I wasn't suggesting that you are either drunk or stupid...I was merely offering you an option"

"I take it we are talking hypothetically?"

"Sure, why not? ... Let's say hypothetically

speaking... What would you do if I was to offer you the next number? ... One, single number and all in." She smiled that beautiful 'trust me' smile, and in a hushed voice she whispered "The next one will be black 31"

And sure enough, the ball settled in black 31

"See, believe me now"

"Ok, so what's the catch?"

"Does there have to be one?" She said casually crossing her legs revealing the thigh split in her full-length dress and with it as much flesh as was humanly possible. The guy was drooling and his tongue all but hanging out, but for all that he still had a modicum of sense.

"There usually is" he replied with a hint of 'I'm not falling for this shit.' I'm glad he thinks he's not, because from where I'm standing, he has fallen for it hook, line and sinker.

She leant back on her stool, took out a gold tipped black cigarette and lit it. There are no smoking signs everywhere.

"See, I can do what I like; I'm the owner. Now, you try lighting a cigarette, and see how long it takes, before you are thrown out on your arse... I would reckon about 90 seconds between you lighting it and you hitting the kerb. So, I ask again... Does there have to be a catch?"

"No, I guess there doesn't have to be but I'm certain you will want something in return"

"Only that you don't go anywhere else"

"So, let me get this straight, you are willing to give me the next number, if I bet all in as long as I don't spend any of it in any other casinos... Right?"

She walks her fingers along his thigh almost purring in his ear "More or less... Yes... Do you want the number?"

Right about now, I'm wondering if he's gonna cum in his pants, or if he already has as he breathlessly murmurs "Yes"

"Red 7...trust me"

"Ladies and Gentlemen place your bets please" I have said that a thousand times to losers like this guy.

Dutifully he places every single chip he owns on red number 7. I spin the wheel, and at this point I almost feel for him... Men! If only they could think from the waist up. Or at least listened, when women spoke to them. We were gonna be

74

seeing a lot more of this guy than he thought, as I believe the exact phrase had been…

"Only that you don't go anywhere else." And by that she meant 'Anywhere else!'

And all it took to lose his freedom…his life and ultimately his soul …was just one more spin of the wheel.

XI STRENGTH

STRENGTH
She Opened the Book for Me – Humberto Maggi

It all started on the day I made the solemn vow. I drifted through the small and dirty streets at the center of Rio de Janeiro, past the avenue Marechal Floriano, where the second-hand bookshops were. Here you could find old books; ones that held the secrets of Quimbanda, intercalated with the Macumba stores, which contain devilish images of Exus and Pomba Giras, red candles and fumigations. Usually, I loved the end of the day in the city, but today, I sensed an inexplicable feeling of oppression. I visited the Church of Santa Rita de Cássia and sat in the cool nave for at least half an hour. In the past, I had used the knowledge I had gathered from perusing obsessively the Book of Saint Cyprian to enlist the souls of the dead slaves buried there in my sorcery.

The cool air inside the church slightly alleviated the oppressive sensation and I had a moment of clarity. I understood now that I had left the initiatory process for far too long; I had forgotten that very specific frame of mind that arises from the conscience when we are following a path with signposts, ordeals and achievements. I had wholly dedicated myself for years only to the horizontalization of my experiences, where the initiated was progressively substituted by the sorcerer. All I wanted was to go deeper and deeper into the knowledge and have conversations with the demons and the dead.

I suddenly felt that the time left was on the verge of not being anywhere near enough for me to achieve the next elusive step. The oppressive energy that surrounded me outside the church was the result of the necromantic energy I had been tapping into, repeatedly; all over the city. I knew the secrets of the cemeteries and churches of Rio de Janeiro, the power at the best of the crossroads. I had a room full of images from Quimbanda, where dozens of red and black candles burned all the time. There was nowhere else for me to go on this path, that I could see. I would have to waste the rest of my days maintaining the balance of what I had already achieved; I had reached the limit of my power and potential in these practices.

That was the moment I spontaneously made the solemn vow. What happened next was remarkable. There was a "clear silence" for an instant and then the world "shifted its angle." I don't know how to describe it, but it was as if I had been standing on a firm base that had suddenly rotated to one side; this base however, was the entire world.

I left the church and took a long look and a deep breath. I had to adjust, to exactly what I was perceiving: two realities, or two levels of reality? Either way, they were juxtaposed right in front of my eyes. It was like being in an oneiric landscape built from the memories of a place. I had often dreamt that the center of Rio de Janeiro was filled with different places and streets; those which I was unable to find when awake; this dream 'place,' had now appeared combined with the city I was so familiar with.

The city of Rio de Janeiro had been built on the blood of slayed Native American Indians and African Slaves. It had a century's worth of sorcery; a port city which opened to everything and everyone. It had been such a long time, since I read the notable words of another lover of this city; words that had been written at the beginning of the 20th century:

When they read the great newspapers, the people imagine they are in an essentially Catholic country, where some mathematicians are positivists. However, the city swarms of religions. Just stop at any corner, ask questions of passers-by and the diversity of the worship and religious services will astonish you. There are Swendeborgeans, literary pagans, physiologists, defenders of exotic dogmas, authors or reformers of Life, revelators of the Future, Devil lovers, blood drinkers, descendants of the Queen of Sheba, Jews, schismatics, Spiritists, babalaos from Lagos, women who respect the ocean, all the cults, all the beliefs; all the forces of the scare and the scarred, who, through the calmness of their countenance, will divine the tragedies of their souls? Who in his quiet walk among men without passions will discover the revelations of new rites, magicians, neuropaths, the delirious, those possessed by Satan, the mystagogues of Death, the secrets of both the Sea and the Rainbow? Who will be able to perceive, in conversing with these creatures, the fratricidal struggle because of the interpretation of the Bible, the struggle that makes a thousand religions wait patiently for Jesus, whose reappearance is marked for any of these days, and waiting for the Antichrist, who may already be walking among them? Who will imagine distinguished gentlemen in intimacy with the disembodied souls, who will unravel the conversations with the angels in the fetid dandies? [1]

And now, this half-hidden aspect of the city, full of cannibals and calibans had been opened to me after my solemn vow. I tried to close my eyes, but it made no difference! I could see it all with my eyes open or shut.

I walked the street, gradually becoming accustomed to the double reality, or the double vision of the reality. Was this a psychotic episode? Some wild flashback or past experience?

I felt compelled to stop in front of the old books store; there was something important there. In the normal world the place is known as Elizart Livros; but in this alternative reality the brownish plaque on the front now reads Art of Eli. At first glance it was the same familiar bookstore, smelling of old tomes. But upon closer inspection, I noticed that somehow, the store was now longer and deeper than I remembered it to be.

There was also a flickering light coming from a room at the far end of the bookshelves.

I walked into the corridor lined by old books of every sort; some of them glimmered in an array of different colours as I passed by. I wondered if their shine came from the inherent power of their contents, or whether it was reminiscent of the energy left by the previous owner or owners?

In the room at the back of the store a rite was being performed.

There were three men, two standing and one sitting reading an old book that gave the appearance of being inexpensive, and a two-meter-tall white candle, that looked to be made of human fat that was illuminating the reading.

It was one of the booklets on Quimbanda published at the beginning of the 20th century. I had collected them all; the entire set was written by an anonymous writer using a pseudonym which nobody has ever identified. However, the one they were reading in a magical way was unknown to me. Let me be more specific: it had never been published on our normal side of the reality. It told of an Exu King I never heard of before, from a Quimbanda Kingdom I did not know.

I left the place feeling dizzy, why was I being shown these things? When would these visions or dreams end?' I almost bumped into the large black man waiting on the sidewalk in front of the bookshop. He had a big and peaceful smile; I knew him to be a spirit because he looked far more real and vivid then anyone or anything else. His clothes were the simple vestment of the slave; white shirt and trousers, I sensed he was the spirit of an African prince prior to the slave trade, and someone whose life had been cut short on this street. He was now the very soul of the street, and his face appeared to be covered in colored tapestries and I understood he was much more than he had first appeared, he was an Egungun of all the slaves buried there.

I felt a little guilt many times before for assessing the souls buried in front of the church, but now the spirit was there reassuring me that I had done something good for them. I had offered them work and I had paid with light and with blood, the two things that mattered to them, and I had never asked for an evil deed to be carried out by them. 'This is why you will do good in the abyss.' – he said putting his hands on my shoulders.'

80

At that moment the world shifted again, and something in my mind clicked, like when a piece of machinery fits into another. I could still see both realities but now the "normal" one had become clearer, sharper. Everything else was still there, I could see the unseen, but it was now in a secondary position...

A voice spoke inside me, the voice of a girl. I saw it was a part of my mind speaking for itself! She said, 'Don't forget the hidden room.' The Hidden Room?

During the most difficult times of my life I rented an apartment in the old and impoverished downtown area near the Saara commerce neighborhood, and the Campo de Santana. It was more than thirty years ago but the building I had lived in back then was the center of my oneiric Rio de Janeiro; that ghost of a city with its divergent architecture which was now visible to my newly awakened eyes. When I lived there, I named the building The Tower of the Moon.

I could not remember or understand why this memory returned at this moment. Where I lived now was an apartment faraway in Flamengo. It was there where the hidden room existed, in my dreaming experience; but now I knew the room was real, a black and red room with a big book closed upon a small column. The book I have being trying to open my entire life.

I came back home, to see the entrance of the room as a black painted rectangle in the wall. I had to shift position several times in order to be at the correct angle to see the space inside. I had to move sideways to pass through the tight entrance. The room was dismal, an abandoned and neglected place; now and then some images could be weakly seen on the walls, mimicking the "Chambre des Cauchemar" Crowley had in Cefalu; a place I had visited in my youth.

I could not open the book. I did not have the strength necessary for the task and I never would have; I now realized this. The book was not an actual book. It was merely the appearance of one; it was seen by other people at other times in different ways:

to an African hunter of the 14th century it was a red egg with a stony shell; a Greek girl from the dark ages before Homer saw it as a dragon head laying in the bottom of a cave; in Renaissance Europe it was indeed seen by a few as a book, but for others it was a door.

My mistake, since the beginning, was to try to open it by myself. That was something nobody could do: open this mystery by himself or herself. Nobody has the necessary strength; someone else would have to do it for you.

The black wall behind the book became diffused and I could see my old place at the Tower of the Moon. It was a window into the past, to a moment when I had opened the Second Aethyr with much more success than I had noticed at the time. That moment had led me to this present moment; I was in a time loop and could walk through the wall and stand beside of my younger self. Now I could see everything that I had not been able to see back then.

I could see the ghost of the dead prostitute by my side. I had seen her alive a few times, passing by the Praça Tiradentes; we had looked at each other, smiled at each other, but I had never approached her. I had never known of her death, but her spirit came to me and she was there when I called the Aethyr. I guess she did not have much good in her life; her last thoughts included me, and the magic within that room had brought her spirit to me. She was taken by the whirlwind of the energies I had invoked yet had barely noticed it happening. The magic though, had been strong enough to open a crack in time and connect the two moments.

I walked backwards to the black room. I was again looking to the book that was not a book; a mystery I could neither open nor solve. Behind it was the transfigured ghost of the dead prostitute, now a being of magic in the retinue of the Quimbanda.

She seemed happy.

Perhaps, the odd smile or nod was enough to acknowledge her, without judgement or condemnation. These random acts of genuine kindness can give strength to the troubled soul. And now in this reality she could repay my kindness.

She opened the book for me.

---

1 - "As Religiões do Rio", by João do Rio, published in 1904

XII THE HANGED MAN

THE HANGED MAN
Influenced Emotions - Defoe Smith

I've been here so many times before:
I have laughed, I have cried,
I have loved, I have hated
I have birthed and killed for thousands of years.
I've fought and surrendered
more times than I could ever possibly count.
I've starved and gorged myself
by an astronomical amount.

I've seen stars fade to nothing
in an ancient blackened Sky.
I have been there when the heavens caught fire
and the Romans ruled the land.
I have been so close to quitting,
when life seems way, way, way too hard
but I've never forged a future knife,
by drawing a tarot card.

I've felt the pain of being wrong,
because I have never listened to advice.
I have never surveyed the lay of the land
and I've been lost through fear of maps.
The mistakes I've made are the classes I attend;
they sometimes make me weep.
Hot milk, datura and buttercup,
sleep me beauty sleep.

Now watch the magician carefully;
you will still miss his sleight of hand.
Tread softly over wheaten fields;

try not to tread on the fleeing rats.
Now watch the magician's trick over;
diversionary tactics over state.
Practice the manoeuvres repeatedly,
but don't you stay up too late.

I'm the voice that dissuades decisions,
I rest when nothing is said.
I am the feeling in your stomach;
impending doom on high alert.
Now you've got that doubtful feeling,
can't go forward and can't go back,
You are walking down a pavement.
but you mustn't stand on the cracks.

So, keep yer eyes peeled and stay on highest alert;
They have seen what you are getting,
and your plans they will harm.
It won't even matter
if the breakfast is on view,
the card has been drawn
and it is pointed at you.

Eenie, meenie, miney, mo,
the traitors hanging by his toe.
He's left here stinking
for twelve days or more
swaying to and fro.
Suspended and swaying
stuck here for all time,
by the ear or the foot
though slower than the neck
The crows they'll torment
and his eyes they will peck.

XIII DEATH

DEATH
The Ferryman - Diane Narraway

Working on the premise,
Things are never as they seem,
I kept all my fingers crossed
That this was just a dream,
Because a cold dark riverbank,
Had replaced my cosy bed,
And now it would appear, there's a damn good chance I'm dead!

And it didn't take me long
To realise I was not alone,
Or that we were all about to reap
Exactly what we'd sown,
And judging by the crowd
It had been a busy night,
Which was of little consolation as the ferry came in sight.

And when it finally reached the shore
A shout came from the crowd,
"Just who the bloody hell are you?"
But the ferryman just bowed,
Tipped his hat! Winked his eye,
And with a flash of his gold crown
Said in a market traders voice,
"Now let's see who's fer goin'up 'n' who's fer goin' dahn!"

Armed menacingly with a clipboard,
And a little stubby pen
He smiled as he scanned the list,
Of those who'd been condemned.

Now when I call out your name,"
His smile broadened to a grin,
"You can rest assured you'll be paying for your sin!

Firstly! Perverts and fornicators,
Especially you…Your grace,
'Cos for members of the clergy,
We can always find a space.
For there are few worse crimes,
than those who claim to teach,
Others how-to walk-in truth, yet don't practice what they
preach!

Next up…those who've taken human life
Without just cause or reason!
'Cos the slaughter of the innocent
Is universal treason,
And one man's terrorist…
Is not another's freedom fighter!
Dress it up how you like, your sentence won't be lighter!

As for those who took the bottle
Or the needle as their wife,
Hell won't seem too far removed
From that which you called life
But you should be aware,"
He said with a smirk
"The drugs they sell down here *REALLY* just don't work.

Now, as for liars, thieves and petty crooks
Who broke the law for kicks;
We have made some room for you,
Across the river Styx.

Although every now and then 'tis said
He turns a blinded eye,
To the petty misdemeanours of those just trying to get by.

Ah! Jehovah's witnesses, you're on my list.
For all that door to dooring.
And the Mormons just because
The book of Mormon is so boring.
And as for the rest of you!
Don't think you are exempt.
There's more of you going down. You're an easy race to tempt."

My knees weren't just knocking,
They were banging,
Like a bishop in a brothel!
Cos, I felt sure he'd call my name,
And I'd be bound for hell!
And whether I was dreaming,
Or if in fact had died,
Didn't seem to matter much stood on that river side.

And though relief swept over me
When he put down his list.
I still blurted out, "Excuse me, sir,
I think I have been missed.
'Cos I'm sure in all honesty
If you look again,
Under 'Sinners Miscellaneous' I'm sure you'll find my name."

"Tell me foolish little child,
Do you suppose I cannot read?
Just what do you think you're guilty of?
Explain your evil deed!
'Cos no one ever gets past me

Not since the dawn of time
And luckily for you right now stupid questions aren't a crime!

Consider yourself lucky,
Your name is nowhere to be seen.
You must 'ave been forgiven
And your slate has been wiped clean.
However, those whose names I've called,
Make sure you have your fare.
For if you cannot pay, you'll be swimming over there.

'Cos there are no free rides,
As I'm sure you have been told.
And American Express will not do nicely!
We only deal in gold!!
But those still standing on the shore,
Who are bound for Paradise,
Have already paid in full, by simply being nice.

For none of you can truly say
You could not tell wrong from right.
Or honestly believed 'free will'
Meant do what the fuck you like!
So, if by chance you should wake,
To find this was all a dream,
It would be to your advantage, to remember all you've seen.

And always be *real* careful
Of the path you choose,
'Cos trust me when I say to you,
This ain't no pleasure cruise.
So, buckle up real tight
And hang on to your hats now ladies
'Cos this here ferry's turbo charged, 'n' my next stop is Hades!"

XIV

S. Vine

XIV TEMPERANCE

TEMPERANCE
The Moratorium - Sem Vine

Mora's skin protested against the cold, moon-dusted air as she opened the back door. Gooseflesh, futile remains of an ancient existence, lighted the rawness of her sunburn, prickled at the scrapes from the day's battle with brambles and ivy. She breathed deeply the dark, sweet scent of broken soil and torn weeds, admiring the progress she had made that afternoon when an unseasonable heat had kindled in her an impulse to clear some wild from her garden. The soreness of her skin and the aching beyond it simply widened her smile of satisfaction.

Stepping out into the sleeping world, the night dew grasped her shoeless feet with an icy touch. Tiny stones clung to the wriggling dampness of her toes as she entered the relative warmth of the shed, soft, woody, grave-like, blue in the fullness of the moon. Something shone, a fox screamed, and Mora bathed in contentment. She lit the rusting lamp and the cobalt night fled through the spidered window, ran shyly into corners and into every shadow, as Mora took her place before the mirror.
She paused for the familiar pair of inkish eyes, gaze dancing one to the other, then following the starbursts of furrows that bled from them like sunrays.

The feet of crows, they call them...

...channels for the joy and tears of the Trickster's work, evidence of the light too light and the dark too dark, bearing no trace of which was which, just that 'things' passed this way, along the pathways for the cunning...

...A breeze breathed through the night's stillness, bringing the scent of jasmine and the sea-like sound of a million leaves. Mora, distracted, wondered if she had heard whispers of long-gone angels, but movement in the mirror called her back to follow the trails and trials of a life. Her lips, she saw, had dried from denying the thirst her body had declared in the sun. She remembered the plumpness of their youth and saw in the mirror the mouths of the youths that had kissed them, how she had turned them away and fed their memories to the ground. She saw their thin-lipped frowns and their teeth-filled curses.

But you're still here. All of you.

Though Mora felt little but the chill of the small hours, the mirror revealed pale hands that caressed the tangle of her hair, her browned neck, the swell of her belly and the curve of her thigh. For all the world, the quivering of the spotted glass would have been the unsteady lamplight, and the subtle ripples ebbing and flowing over the worm-pocked frame would have been the shadows of moths.

When the sky turned lilac as the early light veiled the stars and the passerines sang to the strawberry sun, Mora smothered the lamp's fading flame with the dew on her fingers, while the mirror held captive the last of the moon.

Tea.

Passing the stones she had so recently freed, each etched by her histories and marking a past she could perpetually exhume, she reverently loved them with the gentlest of sighs, and closed her back door on the morning.

XV THE DEVIL

THE DEVIL
The Invocation of my Demon Sister
Lou Hotchkiss Knives

"You can't escape.

I know exactly how to fasten the collar, pin you down by the throat and choke you till dark stars start dancing before your eyes and you collapse in a heap. Only then do I unleash my rage.

You know my roar only too well. It jars in your ears and penetrates everything, planting death at the core of every seed of innocence. You say it sounds like madness, or like the death of a child. You say you've heard it enough, but will you ever have what it takes to shut me up? You are a coward. For half of your life I have ripped and raped and torn and destroyed everything you hold most dear. I have stood in your way like an unfathomable wall, blocking the way to everything that is good and true. Go ask Alice, the one who sold her arse for acid, I am both the Labyrinth and the Beast at its heart.

I lurk under your windows at night as you toss and turn in your bed, haunted by the vague old shadows, mere rumours of my presence. You can feel me coming a mile off, but you never know when I will attack. Sometimes months or even years pass without the faintest hint of my presence. I like to lull you into a false sense of security. I will never leave you alone. I will always be back for you.

There are those who swear they will slay me, who hold vainglorious dreams of rescuing you. But because you are blind, they will never try hard enough. How could they, when you know full well they have fed me day after day, sometimes for years, from the crumbs of the banquets they have held in honour of the tyrants of the Earth? They were once the bullies, the cowardly bystanders, the betrayers, the shallow fresh-faced cads. All of them, at one time of another, were me. The fools, they have been feeding my kind since the beginning. They have no idea how complicit they are.

Forget their promises, everything they say will inevitably end up sounding like lies to your ears. They will slam doors in frustration. They will try to reason with you, cry tears of blood for you, but it will be too little, too late. In turn, you are the one who will abandon them. I love a little bitter irony.

There are no healers, my dear. All the King's horses and all the King's men, all the lovers and all the concerned mothers in the world could never make you whole again. They were doomed before the battle even began. I will wait for the cracks to appear in their armour and I will strike. You will watch them crumble to the floor and turn away in disgust. They will inevitably disappoint you.

No one can save you.

I am the Father of Life and I eat my children alive. I am black like atomic rain, both the Mother and Creation of a world based on oppression, competition and ownership. I am without and within, the Challenger they call the Devil because they recognise the divinity of my Infernal nature.

I AM Nature, a savage and never-ending story of hunters and hunted, the moment when the flame of existence extinguished in the eyes of the gazelle, the law that dictates that predators should eviscerate those unfortunate enough to have been born at the bottom of the food chain.

You can't escape.

I know exactly how to fasten the collar, just loose enough so you could easily remove it. But you never remove it. You are scared of what life would be without me. You have forgotten to be free. You cannot even imagine what that would feel like. So, you have resigned yourself to a life of servitude.

So far, you are a failure. And so, I return, again and again, to your ageing carcass, in the hope that one day, you will finally understand. But, my accursed fool, my terrified slave, you never do. So, when you hear me growl at night, and wonder why the moon is dull and the air foul, remember this; I have no intention of ever letting you go.

I am simply trying to get a different reaction, time after time.

See? The black stars are dancing before your dying eyes. If only you would notice how loose that collar is."

XVI THE TOWER

THE TOWER
The Lay of Dahut of Ys - Lou Hotchkiss Knives

Imagine the place you love most in the world. The place where your heart is truly and utterly at peace, where you feel perfectly safe; the place that, at some stage in your life, no matter the reason, forever bound your soul to its beauty and history.

That place is the place I lost.

Imagine, on the coast of Brittany, a jewel standing in that liminal area between earth, sea and sky. A walled city with white walls that gleamed in the sun, and dozens of towers, their rooves tiled with a mosaic of blue and grey slate, rare obsidian and lapis lazuli. Imagine small gardens that, despite the harsh Atlantic winds, somehow magically brim with greenery - Camélia, Roses, clematis, apples, ornamental artichokes and vegetables. Imagine musicians on every street corner, shops thriving, artists sharing, poets courting inspiration. Picture a kind of golden age Dolce Vita; a diet plentiful with fish and sea-borne delicacies, distilleries exporting a delicious brand of algae liquor, and add to that, amidst the population, a very certain flair for street elegance.

Before this idyllic scene stretched the white sands of Breizh, and, beyond that, fields jewelled with standing stones and crowned by verdant forests. Around and behind the city, the mighty Ocean, depending on His mood, sighed, growled, or whispered. We revered Him. The Ocean and the Earth were our sovereigns. We were but living testimonies to their magnificence.

That was Ys. That was the place I lost.

Chapter 1
The Worm in the Fruit

Some people say that prior to birth, our unborn souls choose their parents as well as the challenges individually inherent to each incarnate life.

I chose a life of privilege that I was not to keep. I was the only child of Granelon, king of Ys.

My mother, a northern princess, had died on her drakkar on her way to Brittany, as she gave birth to me. Her name was Malgven. As a little orphan girl, I remember begging my father's friends to tell me stories about her. Her name alone was enough to transport me in lands where snow and ice covered the plains and forests in the purest white, where the air was so crisp that cheeks became as red as apples, as red as my mother's hair; and where the proximity of bodies made up for the constant hegemony of the cold.

My father was what the people call a fair ruler, kind, large when needed, and a good listener, who loved to visit his people and take an active interest in their everyday lives.

Privately, he was a languishing widower who was somewhat aloof and overly sentimental. With hindsight, I recognise his altruism made him easily influenced, and I certainly, when he was alive, abused his generosity and love for me.

I was far from the epitome of the great daughter. I was spoilt and haughty, vain and self centered. Looking back, I had no idea how fortunate I was, nor how much I was loved. From my father I took and took, all for granted- jewels, dresses, riches, promises. I didn't give back much. All that mattered to me was my beautiful self. My portraits, the parties I gave. The lovers I took.

Ah, my lovers. There were many, ranging from the humblest, fresh faced sailors to the most daring explorers and prestigious merchants. Reader, some will no doubt poison your ear about my crimes, and I have committed many; but this much is true: I have loved each one of them as if he was the living incarnation of all that is good and true. My pagan love rites demanded that I embraced each one once, and only once: the night before they set sail and left the security of Ys to surrender themselves to the arms of my true beloved, Llyr, the mighty Ocean.

To each of them, the Ocean was a fierce rival. Whilst some successfully crossed its storms and relished in its bounty, others never returned. My role was to prepare them for the voyage, one of survival or sacrifice, depending on the Fates.

I was not meant to get attached.

That suited me. I was barely twenty and, although I took my Ocean Priestess duties seriously, I had, in truth, committed myself to a life of carefree, unbridled hedonism. Music, dance, wines, luxurious garnements, pleasure, beauty: Ys provided me with endless opportunities to savour the ecstasy of life, and I seized each day with gleeful anticipation.

It was around that time that a hermit called Corentin, accompanied by a retinue of stern bearded men, came to Ys from the heart of the mainland. In their bags they carried the holy book of a new religion which had been steadily gathering followers in the neighbouring kingdoms. My father, a man open to new currents and ideas, expressed curiosity, and the men were invited to the palace for an audience.

I shudder at the recollection of the day I first heard Corentin's booming voice resound under the blue mosaic arches of the palace. I was sitting next to the King under a dais of gold-embroidered silk of peacock hues. As the men were invited in, we could not help but notice that their hair and clothes were filthy, and that they walked barefoot like vagrants. Corentin, their leader, was a tall man with olive skin and deep, penetrating dark eyes. His nose was narrow and hooked like the beak of a bird of prey, and his cheeks were hollow like those of a man who is used to going hungry. As he walked towards us, I noticed his thin lips curling into a wry smile and, for a fleeting second, I could have sworn I saw a glimpse of disdain flash through his black eyes. Although Corentin looked like a beggar, he appeared utterly unimpressed by the beauty and luxury of the room that surrounded him.

He may as well have been visiting a stable. There was a sinister arrogance in his gaze I found both disrespectful and unsettling.

After bowing deeply before my father, the men went about to expose the principles of their faith. There was, they claimed, only one God, who originated from a dry, inhospitable land near Egypt. That god loved humanity, they claimed, so much that it had sacrificed his only son to save us all from death. Yet the new god was jealous and implacable, and demanded of his followers; absolute submission and unwavering devotion, to the exclusion of any other spirit. Those who refused to embrace the new God's mandatory love would face an eternity of agonising torment in the afterlife.

Such was the Christian faith, promising salvation to the blindly obedient, exalting suffering and austerity, targeting the poor and the disaffected so as to get gradually closer to the high spheres of power.

Despite my objections, my father, following this first audience allowed Corentin and his retinue to settle in Ys. It didn't take long for the intentions of the newcomers to become clear - they were here to take over. Theirs was a well-rehearsed routine, practiced in kingdom after kingdom. They flattered my father for a few months, lauding his wisdom, providing him with valuable contacts with traders from neighbouring Christian nations, advising him on diplomatic matters. Once they had gained his

trust and respect, they started suggesting that the adoption of the new faith by the population of Ys would elevate our country to the summits of power.

My father was reluctant. He cherished our old ways, the heritage of our ancestors, yet his fascination for the new God, and his increasing reliance on the counsel of the Christians deeply troubled me. Corentin hated me, and barely managed to conceal his disdain in public. With hindsight I realise his scorn was, through me, directed at the whole of Ys, our lifestyle, and our values.

In his world, women were to be veiled, and silent in assemblies. I was outspoken, walked bare headed; I sang and danced in public. So did every other woman in town. Ys was carefree, wild, elegant. Ys was passionately pagan, and we naively thought it would last forever. Somehow most people fooled themselves into thinking they could simply cohabitate with the newcomers, who would just have to learn to accept our ways of life. I didn't share their optimism.

One cannot tolerate intolerance. If one does so, tolerance dies.

Chapter 2
The Oracular Island of Sein: Two Years Later.

A gentle rain was falling as we boarded my barge, which was moored on the beach. Scanning once again the inhospitable landscape, all I could see was pebbles, rocks, and stones standing lonely under the fierce Atlantic winds. Here and there, scrawny bushes with tortured limbs were a testament to the hostility of the elements. The island was small and almost bare, bar a few Fishermen's houses and a tavern, huddling around a small jetty. The crossing had been rough. The reefs around Sein were reputed to be particularly treacherous, and we had taken great risks in undertaking this journey, especially at this time of year. To think we were now going to brave the tumultuous waves once again, especially after what I had heard from the Nine Senanes, only added to the gloomy atmosphere surrounding the crew.

No one knows precisely when the Nine Oracles first settled in Sein, but the ancient megaliths that flanked the door of the sanctuary dated back to a time far anterior to the fall of Atlantis. As far as History could recall, there had always been nine priestesses on the island, and generation after generation from all fringes of the known world had braved the storms to seek the wisdom of their prophecies.

As I took my place on the deck, wrapped in furs, waiting for the sailors to launch our vessel, my mind wandered back to the events of the morning.

I had walked alone to the far end of the island, and from there had made my way to the sanctuary, a simple wooden structure surrounded by standing stones and protected by a wall of pebbles. As I had entered the edifice, all I could see was a fire burning on a tripod at the centre of the room. No statues, no flowers, no fineries. Just the bare earth, the hearth, and a platform on which sat nine hooded figures: the Senanes, the oracles of the Atlantic.

Without hesitation I gave the three secret signs of my priestess initiation, thus signifying to the Nine that I had come as a pilgrim and a magician.

"Who cometh?"

The voice seemed to come from nowhere.

"I, Dahut", I replied, "daughter of Granelon and Malgven, priestess of Llyr, keeper of the keys of the Western Gate of Ys."

As I said so, I knelt, hands pressed upon the great white gold keys that hung from a chain on my bosom. Guarding them was my most sacred duty. The bearer of the keys had the power to keep the city safe, or to open its gates to the savagery of the tides; as such, he or she had to be the most trustworthy soul in the Kingdom. My father's decree had made me, by virtue of my birth, their appointed keeper.

Sometimes, in the depths of my soul, I wondered whether I was really worthy of such an honour.

"What do you seek?" came the voice.

Which of them was talking? It was impossible to tell. I swallowed hard, then began.

"Blessed Senanes, men have come to Ys from a foreign land, bringing with them a new faith that seeks to supplant our old ways. I have come to find out what must be done to defeat them."

Silence. For several long minutes, nothing moved in the sanctuary, bar the flames that danced in the hearth and the shadows they cast over the walls. Unsure of what to do, I remained on my knees, senses on alert. Suddenly, the Senanes got up all at once, standing impossibly tall at the front of the platform. In one voice that sounded like millions of voices echoing from the dawn of time, they delivered their answer before the darkness swallowed them:

"Go home, Dahut of Ys. Our world is dying, and no saviour

106

can redeem our people. The floodgates will open, and the sea will turn red. Our last twilight hath come."

A death sentence! That was the last thing I had expected to hear from the Nine. I had come seeking the advice of our most holy women, the very ones one I would have expected to lead the fight against those who willed to crush our freedom. Yet the Senanes had surrendered without a fight.

At least an hour passed before I found the courage to stand up again.

I returned to Ys anxious and despondent, my hair humid and brittle with salt, my clothes heavy with sea spray, my soul in turmoil. Immediately upon arrival, I demanded an audience with my father to inform him of the outcome of my consultation with the Oracle. To my horror, he dismissed my concerns; worse, he even dared question the authority of the Nine Senanes, arguing they were merely exploiting gullible pilgrims with outdated superstitious practices. There was, he claimed in a misguided attempt to reassure me, nothing to fear - theirs was a creed of no moral or theological value, and their gods were false deities, primitive emanations that still demanded human sacrifices.

My bones shook. Those were not his words; he, the experienced ruler, the curious mind, the free thinker, was now merely parroting the sermons of my enemies. My father, my once wise father had now had his mind poisoned, and all my cajoling or reasoning was now falling on deaf ears. King Granelon had started turning his back on the faith of his ancestors, on his only daughter, and on his people. The change seemed inexorable.

The twilight hath come. Our world is dying.

For days after that, fear gnawing at my flesh, I paced my quarters to and fro, wringing my hands constantly, unable to eat or rest. The perspective of the loss of our homeland felt unbearable, unfathomable. At night my mind kept wandering to the words of the Senanes. Was all hope truly lost? Maybe the prophecy was not meant to come true for a long time. Maybe I would be dead before those ghastly basilicae came to replace the marble temples of the Ocean, before the songs of my fellow women were finally silenced. Maybe Corentin, who now called himself the first Bishop of Ys, would have me murdered.

This last possibility offered, somehow, the glimpse of an uneasy comfort, the fantasy of a cowardish escape, a perspective still much preferable to that of the cataclysm that lay ahead.

How had I, Dahut of Ys, found myself at the heart of this tragedy, not as a political actor, but as a mere hapless spectator? Looking through the window of my room at the gleaming towers of slate and lapis-lazuli, and, further in the distance, at the great Western Gates cradled by the crashing sea; I hanged my head in shame, my aching throat filled with tears.

Chapter 3
The Red Knight

When I was a little girl visiting Britain, I saw, in the palace of King Bran, a curious statue which, I was told, came from faraway Rome. It represented a small child with bird wings attached to his back, holding a bow and arrow. He was, the king had explained, a god of Love, the incarnation of a fierce, blind, uncontrollable force before whom the whole of Creation bowed. On the base of the statue was an inscription which apparently translated as "The True Master of the World."

Back in Ys I had often wondered about that mysterious foreign god, whose grip over humanity's hearts seemed so different from the sacred, primeval wrath of our Ocean, and from the jealousy of the invisible deity the Christians worshipped. How potent, I pondered, could be the arrows of a child's bow? How innocent was that child? Was Love really the strongest force in the universe? The tender lust I felt for each of my beautiful mariners was quickly forgotten the second the silhouette of their ships disappeared over the horizon.

My devotion to the Ocean was anchored in spiritual awe, an elevated unravelling of the soul, very different from human love. At 23, I had heard much about passion, mainly through the stories of the bards who, at the time, travelled from city to city singing tales of tangled lives and star-crossed lovers. Despite this, I knew not what passion truly meant.

All was to change with the coming of the Red Knight.

The second I cast eyes upon his perfect face, I felt reborn. It was as if the vast, vivid morning sky had engulfed itself whole into my soul, burning away the person I had, until then, thought I had been, destroying my values and ideals, and tormenting me with new, unspeakable delights. I was dizzy, yet my body stood stiff and straight; I felt shocked, suspended in time, but my heart was palpitating, my head rushing. For all my brocades and silk outfit, I felt naked and vulnerable. His was a devastating beauty, more dangerous than all the storms of the Atlantic, a cataclysmic catalyst that would shake my existence to its very core.

Even now, after all these years, I can perfectly recall the moment the Red Knight rode through our gates, mounted on a horse which seemed to dance rather than amble, clad in an armour encrusted with rubies and garnets, his gauntlets and boots adorned with swirls of gold. Almost naturally, the crowd had parted on each side of him with murmurs of intrigued reverence. That man was something to behold. Dark haired and azure-eyed, his lovely face, framed by a close-cropped beard, exuded all the vitality of his youthful virility. He could not have been much older than me, yet his demeanour, his whole posture oozed the kind of natural confidence borne from careful training and education.

When he eventually rode past me, magnificent and proud, my heart leapt to my lips, yet I could not utter a word. As I watched him guide his steed up the cobbled avenue, alongside the sun-drenched houses, and disappear up the hill towards the palace, I felt my heart being crushed under the weight of a feeling I can only describe as helpless despair.

To my grief, he had not looked at me once. I had no idea who he was, yet I knew, at that moment, viscerally, that the mere sight of him had already sealed my fate.

That night I came home transfigured, ecstatic, consumed by the most delicious of torments. Febrile with expectation, I immediately enquired if a Knight in red armour had announced himself at the entrance of the palace, but, to my disappointment, the guards assured me no such person had reported to the gates that day. That night, however, two of my maids, whom I had sent to town in hope of gleaning information, returned with the news that the stranger had indeed, been seen around Ys that evening, and that he was already, unsurprisingly, the talk of the town.

From tavern to harbour to salon, men speculated, women swooned, and rumours ran wild. As he was obviously a nobleman of high rank, it was only a matter of time, my maids assured me, before he came to the palace to announce his arrival to the King.

Except that he didn't. A week passed in a maelstrom of alternating despair, wild hopes, painful longing and frustrated desire. By day I was restless, fidgety, driven to distraction; by night, I was haunted by the memory of his beauty, I writhed on my bed, burning with unfulfilled lasciviousness, slumber forever deserting my eyes.

What was happening to me? What god, I wondered, had cursed me so? Had the little winged archer pierced my heart with his devastating arrows in a careless bout of child-like mischief? What for? Was this what the Romans meant when they said that Love was the true master of this world?

Lonely amidst my servants, alone at the mercy of my crushing limerence, I neglected my obligations, abandoning my daily devotions at the altar of the Ocean to dream the days away, constantly reminiscing the brief instant, I had laid eyes upon him. My obsession, by now, was confining to madness. I was ready to abjure my faith, renounce my status, just for a chance to worship before that beloved face and offer myself as a willing sacrifice to the object of my most violent desire. Gone were the memories of my sea voyage and the chilling prophecy of the Senanes, forgotten were the terrors of the past years. Corentin's scorn, his constant plotting, the threat of the new faith didn't matter anymore. My all-devouring infatuation had driven out of my heart all those who had once mattered. The mighty Ocean, my kingdom, my father, Ys itself had ceased to exist.

Love is greater than Nature. It binds and fuels Nature, and, like Nature, it is ruthless, cruel and selfish. But, intoxicated and delirious, I kept plucking the petals of roses, my limbs languid, my bosom heaving with unspent lust, my apostasy complete.

Chapter 4
Beltane

Later that month, I was due to preside, as mandated by birth, over our yearly celebration of the Beltane fires. There was to be a procession through the city, followed by the sacrifice of a white horse on the altar of the Llyr. Then, at nightfall, the townspeople would light bonfires in the streets, and dance around an immense blazing labyrinth in the main square. After that would come the Chase, that long awaited moment when young men and women, elated by the dancing and revelries, would scatter through the narrow streets of the old town, masked and crowned with garlands, each hoping to find a lover amidst the crowd of joyous revellers. Some always did, some struggled, some inevitably returned home alone; but all treated the event with utmost reverence. Such were our ways, life-affirming, joyful, playful. In the past, I had always awaited our Beltane rites with much impatience. To my shame, that year, their spiritual significance had become the least of my concerns. The Chase was just another opportunity to roam the streets in search of the young Knight whose face had never stopped haunting me. I had not slept more than a few hours for nights, yet my body, exhausted by constant pining, still screamed for he, whom I now called my sole Beloved.

That night, as I stood by my father under the royal silk canopy, I cared not for the songs, the devotions, the prayers; later, as the sacrificial Knife was thrust in my hand, my soul, for the first time did not swell in awe at the solemnity of the instant. When I plunged the blade into the throat of the sacrificial stallion, a magnificent beast of pure white, the miracle of life gushing away from the wound failed to elevate my heart. My soul stood bare, lost and numb; I felt nothing, bar a vague annoyance. As the labyrinth was finally lit, my eyes cared not for the brightly coloured paper lanterns, the painted statues, the elaborate pyres of burning sandalwood, the flower and fragrant herbs that strew the path of the dancers. All I wanted was for the formalities to end. So, too, it seems, did my father, whom, sitting next to me, appeared morose and preoccupied. Not that I cared. We had grown distant of late, and I had come to despise his servility to the newcomers' advice.

Feverishly I kept scanning the crowd, desperate for a glimpse of scarlet, the glint of rubies catching the light of the flames.

Finally, as the labyrinth emptied, I hastily bowed before the crowd and disappeared behind the royal tent. After having made sure the great keys to the Western Gate lay concealed under my clothes, I wrapped myself in a coat of ultramarine blue, adjusted over my face an elaborate mask of carved silver, and made my escape into the twilight.

Chapter 5
Floodgates

How long did I roam the streets for, a forlorn pilgrim, limbs on fire, heart wrenched, my mouth turned sore by the constant litany of prayers I addressed to the winged god of Rome, that child-deity whose name I still did not know? By what miracle did the divine bow-bearer eventually lend an ear to my pitiful supplications? After hours of walking, senses on alert but speaking to no-one, I reached the walled gardens that flanked the main sanctuary. Leaving the crowd behind me, I sighed and collapsed, exhausted, onto a stone bench that stood under an arch of roses.

It was then that I finally saw him.

He was even more beautiful than I could recall. The flickering flames of a nearby lantern and the blue hues of the nascent night enhanced further the loveliness of his features. He wore a suit of crimson embroidered with garnets, with a belt of vermillion and gold leather circling his slender hips. As he stood, silent, so close I could almost have touched him, I marvelled drunkenly at the effortless grace of his poise.

Time stopped. The world went silent. The wind abated, the leaves of the great birches stopped rustling, and the stars, far above, held their breath.

Slowly, he turned towards me, and I gasped once more as I beheld the face of my saviour. Finally, our eyes met.

As I rose to him, quivering, faint with shock, I heard him distinctly call my name. His voice seemed otherworldly, as if it came from beyond the veil of existence.

"Dahut" …it repeated, softly. "Dahut…"

I never thought for a second to ask him how he knew who I was.

Chapter 6
Star Crossed

For long minutes we stood in perfect silence.

"…What is your name?" I managed to blurt out eventually, after I plucked the courage to give him my hand to kiss - the long-awaited moment of first contact; so delightful I felt unstable on my feet.

He gave me a mischievous smile and held my gaze intently but did not reply.

"Who are you?" I insisted.

His blue eyes fluttered, his smile widened, I could have sworn he was blushing. Shaking his head, he cupped my chin in his hand and gave me a long kiss, a kiss of such deliciousness it eclipsed every embrace I had ever had until then.

He had me in his grip.

There was a pregnant pause. He tilted his head back, sighed as if taking the heavens for witness, then gazed again into my eyes with all the tenderness in the world. I swooned.

"I am the Devil" he said.

"No, you are far too handsome. Besides, the devil only tempts Christians" I laughed breathlessly, shaking my head.

"Who knows whom the Devil truly serves?" he replied with a wink and a smile.

"Come on" I begged. "What is your real name?"

"I told you already. I am the Devil."

I shrugged and did not question him any further. For tonight, and as long as I could kiss him to my heart's content, the Devil would do. There would be plenty more time to talk in the morning.

Away from the crowd we went, walking alongside the ramparts, arm in arm under a sky extravagant with stars. He didn't speak much, yet I felt comfortable with him, as if I had known him all my life.

To my blissed-out mind, Ys, in the light of the multitude of lanterns that decorated its facades, had never appeared more beautiful.

Its picturesque houses, adorned with soft coloured wisteria or fragrant jasmine, its wells dressed in ribbons and garlands of flowers, its statues of water spirits guarding pumps and fountains - everything, in that moment, was basking in perfection, as if paying homage to the True Master of this World.

Later, as we lay entwined upon my bed, I told him, shedding tears of gratitude, that he had brought me the greatest gift of all: that of Wholeness, a divine treasure one only finds at the end of desire, in the moment of ecstasy when the boundaries between one's Self and the World finally dissolve.

Never had I felt so whole.

Chapter 7
The House of God

I awoke suddenly, bolt upright in the dead of the night. My lanterns had gone out, and I could barely distinguish the faint light that came in from the open arched window in front of me.

Not a star in sight. The air was heavy, and, in the wind, the eventuality of a Summer storm hung like a veiled threat. From outside came a grumbling sound, like that of distant thunder.

As the surreal memories of last evening flooded my mind again, so returned the violent pang of desire. I wanted him again. My Devil, my Red Knight.

My hands groped in the obscurity, searching for my beloved's body across the bed, but as I reached out, my fingers only closed on shadows.

The mattress was cold.

"Where are you?" I called, softly at first, then louder. Where was he, indeed? I sat upon the bed, fumbling cushions, pulling sheets, a blind, naked woman, alone in the dark. Had he gotten up already? Had he left? Not a move, not an answer, nothing to stir the night. The room was absolutely silent, bar the rumbling noise outside.

I dragged myself to the edge of the bed, found the table nearby, stood up and made my way to the door. In the deserted corridor, a single torch, attached to the wall, was still burning. Grabbing it, I returned to my bedroom. It was empty.

Something was not right; I could feel it. Instinctively, my hand went to reach for the heavy gold keys around my neck.

The chain was gone. So were the keys to the Western Gate.

Suddenly alarmed, I started searching the room frantically, first the floor, then the tables, turning over the drawers, tossing jewellery boxes, furiously stripping the bed bare, overcome by panic. Had he left with the keys? No, it could not be. Where was he? Where were the Gate Keys?!

As I was still frenetically rummaging through my belongings, a spine-chilling scream ripped at the fabric of the night. Outside, the grumbling noise had intensified, and I could hear the distinct sound of a commotion, somewhere below my window. What was happening?! More screams followed, and a mounting tumult, as if a crowd was assembling. By now terrified, I darted to the door, before realising I was still naked, except for the vermillion belt of the Red Knight, just barely hanging off my hipbones. Gathering my clothes as fast as I could, I undid the belt, which fell to the ground with a metallic clatter. By the light of the torch, I noticed a pouch was attached to it, which seemed to contain something heavy. The keys? My shaking fingers barely managed to undo the knot around the small bag. It indeed contained a weighty metallic object. But as I pulled it to the light, I realised it wasn't my keys at all.

It was a crucifix.

Chapter 8
Deluge

Somewhere in another world, the sky shattered like glass and its shards rained upon my heart, stabbing me through and through. For an instant, logic withdrew from my mind; my senses blurred, leaving me stunned and silent. As if in a bad dream, I watched myself staring at the bronze cross in my hands, daring not to acknowledge the obvious. Suspended in the eye of the cyclone, I could not have strung a single rational thought together.

The next second, a deafening crash coming from outside snapped me back into the room. Then another crash, followed by more screams. This time, the tone had changed to one of perceptible anguish. There were wails; in the distance, I could clearly distinguish the cries of children. Suddenly, a voice, louder than all the others, emerged from the tumult, and what it said rang in my ears like a death sentence:

"Oh gods, we are all going to drown!"

It was then that the enormity of what had just happened hit me with the full force of a tidal wave, devastating everything in its path.

The bastard! ...

I let out a roar of such rage and despair that it ripped my throat raw. So raw, in fact, that my body, in a reflex, immediately bent forward, and I started coughing up blood. With a violence I had never suspected myself capable of, I hurled the hated crucifix against the wall. The gem-incrusted chain broke instantly, shattering into dozens of pieces, but the cross just bounced against the stone and unto the floor where it disappeared in the shadows.

I ran outside as if possessed, through the megaron and down the corridors until I reached the front terrace of the palace. On the horizon, the night was withdrawing into the dawn, the black sky gradually taking tints of anthracite blue.

A large, terror-stricken group of servants and courtiers was already gathered there, some crying, some screaming.

Still naked and dishevelled, I barged through the hysterical crowd until I found myself at the edge of the balcony.

The vision that offered itself to me was nothing short of nightmarish. Like a gaping wound in the belt of the ramparts, the Western Gate stood wide open, and furious, gigantic waves were gushing in, engulfing everything that stood in their path. The lower part of the town was already gone, debris floating on the surface of the waters, pathetic remnants of the elegant dwellings that had stood there only hours ago.

The area around the Eastern Gate, by contrast, seemed relatively untouched, but we all knew it would be a matter of minutes before the raging Ocean claimed it in its turn. It was now or never.

Like a herd of terrified animals, we made our way through the gardens towards the Eastern Gate. All the while, the water was mounting, each successive wave taking its tribute amongst the streets below, carrying away whole sections of walls, trees, helpless humans and animals whose pitiful cries were lost in the tumult.

Finally, we emerged from the gardens into the walled square that surrounded the Gate, and the crowd let out a cry of triumph. Our relief was to be short-lived.

The Eastern Gate lay wide open. Right before it, on a grey horse, stood Corentin and, riding behind him, ashen-faced and clinging to the Bishop's robe, was my father.

His face was deathly pale, his eyes dilated by shock. He looked so old, so vulnerable. At the sight of him, our once proud pagan King, pathetically grasping onto the coat of the despicable Christian traitor, I let out a scream, but my throat was still so raw I could only produce a muffled growl.

Furiously, I began elbowing my way through the assembled onlookers. "Father! Father!" I called, hoarse and bewildered, desperate to grasp his attention; but my plea was lost amidst the terrible chorus of wails and cries.

With renewed rage I pushed and shoved and clawed my way to the front of the crowd, determined to pull the hated Bishop from his horse and dash his brains upon the cobbles of the street. With a final push, I managed to extricate myself from the human mass, naked, barefoot, grazed and bruised. Corentin saw me first, and, raising his crook, turned to the people, his booming voice barely covering the pandemonium:

"Behold, people of Ys, the whore whose example of debauchery unleashed the wrath of God upon your wretched city!"

"Damn you, traitor! Damn your God! Damn you!" I roared with the last of my breath. Like a Fury I launched myself at the horse, attempting to grab its bridle, determined to kill this bastard Bishop, or die trying. The stallion, startled, reared on its back legs. In a desperate effort I managed to grab its mane, then the pommel of the saddle.

"Father!" I cried again. By now my voice was but a faint rasp, and blood stained my teeth. The cold sweat that poured down my face was burning in my eyes.

"Father!"

Finally, I caught sight of his face. His expression was blank, entirely devoid of emotion. His empty eyes fell upon me.

The unthinkable happened. My father, King Granelon of Ys, shook his head and, pursing his lip in disdain, turned his face away.

My heart sank, my knees buckled underneath me. At that very moment Corentin, raising his crook, took a swing and hit me full force across the face. I felt the bones break, and tumbled backwards on the cobbles, warm blood gushing from my nose and mouth.

The last thing I saw, before the crowd trampled my body, was Corentin and my father exiting through the great Gates, before their followers closed them on the doomed people of Ys.

Chapter 9
The Siren Called Marie Morgane

Sometimes, in the evening, when the mist is so thick it blurs the boundaries between ocean and sky, I hear the wind carry the lament of the dead.

Hundreds of years have passed since the great blue towers of Ys were engulfed under the waves. Their debris, reduced to pebbles and sand by the tide of the years, now lie at the bottom of the sea, unrecognisable to men, their former glory the dregs of a long-forgotten dream.

I had once been a Priestess of the Ocean, pledged to his service, but in doing so I had erred gravely, and my neglect had brought down the most beautiful kingdom of all. I had been entrusted with the sacred keys of my city, those very keys that ensured the continuity of the covenant between the people of Ys and the might of the sea; yet I had failed to protect both the keys and my subjects. The price I pay is one of incommensurable grief, especially on those nights the wailing dead rise from the sea, forever bemoaning the loss of the homeland they loved. They know I am still amongst them, although I am now of a different nature.

What the Christians never understood was that our gods were not devoid of mercy.

For all my faithlessness, the Ocean never abandoned me. I roam its depths, a siren-like, wandering soul caught between the world of spirits and that of animals, my song hanging over the water when the sea is still.

I hear other voices, too. The polyphonic oracles of the Nine still hang around the arid rocks of the isle of Sein, albeit faintly. If men could learn to lend an ear, they would hear them herald a new age, one bloodied by wars and violence, one that may finally bury the aberration of monotheism.

This said, I am more interested, these days, in the voices of the dying. Sweet boys as pale as roses, toppled by storms into the open jaws of Llyr, the all-devouring Ocean. I hold them in my arms as they fight death with jerking limbs, as if in the throes of ecstasy. I marvel as they expire, powerless, suddenly so poignantly fragile at the excruciating moment the soul wriggles free from the flesh. There was a time when I made love to the living. One time I embraced the Devil. Now I tenderly cradle those who depart.

On Summer nights I lie at the crest of the waves, my body stretched to the limits of water and sky, my long algae hair forming a blue halo around me, dreaming the twilight. I always gaze at the same star, the brightest one. Long ago, when I was still Dahut of Ys, a dark-haired youth in a crimson armour told me that star's name was Venus.

I have since learned that, in the morning, that bright orb is the last star to fade away.

Men call it Lucifer.

XVII THE STAR

THE STAR
Mortal Gods - Diane Narraway

Once there had been many of us, loved above all others or so they say; the past being little more than a hazy memory these days. I remember our parents, but they died long ago and now it is just myself and my twin sister. I've heard there are more of us: brothers and sisters who also fled the massacre, but as yet, neither of us have seen any. It is a different world these days but in truth the people seem much the same as they always have been. Some intuitive, some ruthless, some still fearing a god that has been dead for millennia.

As I recall, there was a war, followed by several other wars and those seeking a new order and a new era, were both brutal and bloodthirsty. The event that killed our parents is one of the few clear memories I still have. They came in the night; the battle had raged on for so long that many wondered if it would ever end. And if it ended what then, would the victory be worth the sacrifice made by either side. It ended with the slaughter of both my father and mother and we ran for our lives. We survived but at what cost?

We hid for many years and our names were so maligned, dripping like curses from the tongues of those 'others' shunned by their communities. We wondered back then if we would ever be an acceptable part of this new world; one that seemed hell bent on slandering our once good names. We had been beautiful once but lies, and curses can damage even the purest of souls and in doing so those once considered beautiful become portrayed as grotesquely hideous.

People are funny though. The mere mention of the word god, whether it has a capital G or not, and they instantly assume them to be immortal. What if they aren't? Few consider this and even less believe it. In fact, the notion of no deity seems easier for them to accept than a deity with a life span. The truth of the matter is that deities are created, exist and die and people are the cause.

Now, only myself, and a handful of my siblings have survived. Why? The simple truth is we were not the only ones condemned to hide in the shadows in order to survive, there is many a down-trodden soul here with us: drunks, drug addicts, convicts, whores and above all Wytches.

Wytches, those intuitive and gifted members of the community whose bloodline like ours cannot be wiped out, nor can it be silenced, and their belief is all it took. It wasn't easy as they too spent many years being tortured, incarcerated and all too often murdered. All in the name of a god! Better still a god that had been dead for many, many years! This new order is several overthrown gods down the line and those who killed my parents are long forgotten, yet our names are still heard; no longer as curses but as names with power. It began with the hushed whispers of Wytches as they weaved their spells and performed their sacred rites. Gaining momentum in the world of secret societies and all those desperately seeking something to believe in, in a world that had lost its way.

And how it will end I don't know. However, what I do know is that slowly and surely the world is awakening; myself, my sister along with some of our other siblings who also escaped grow stronger every day. These latest gods have no substance and are born out of material greed and fear, and the spirit of this world is suffering as they struggle to maintain their grip on society. The world has lost so much but there is always hope as more and more people wake up to the morning star.

XVIII THE MOON

THE MOON
Forever Wild - Esme Knight/Diane Narraway

The howl rose like the full moon. It echoed above the canopy of the forest and bounced off the surrounding mountains. Below, shrouded in the darkness a silhouette slipped through the trees, silent and unseen. The hooded figure stopped for a moment inclining their head towards the sound. It could not be far now. The ragged cliff faces, and dense woodland made it difficult to Judge; their prey could be higher up on the mountain side and to climb the steep face would be impossible at night even in the moonlight. They continued to stalk through the wood hoping that the beast would be closer to the ground. Returning empty handed was not an option, there was more than just a matter of pride at stake, perhaps even a life hung in the balance. Her life.

Stories had always been told of how bold young women were tempted and enticed away into the woods during the harvest full moon, as if a blood-tithe must be paid for the bounty reaped. Nobody ever explained what had tempted them, it was simply referred to as the Howling. Over time, the Howling had become little more than an excuse for the Elders to send those they viewed as feisty or troublesome, or simply those they did not care for, into the wood as punishment.

Punishment for what wasn't always clear but none the less they sent at least one girl every year. Some returned cowed, eyes never leaving the ground and were quickly married. Some returned with an inner madness and were cast out beyond the edge of the village, to remain spinsters until their final breath. Some did not return at all.

They could call it what they liked it was the women that intrigued the Hunter; more specifically those who did not return. Where did they go? Were they captured, enslaved? Eaten? And if so, by what? Was the beast just a fairy story to scare little girls into what they believed was "nice behaviour," maybe originally it had been to warn them of the dangers that could befall a little girl lost in the forest. Or was there perhaps a kernel of truth in it somewhere? Or did these poor girls just run away to find a better life? One less judged perhaps? These questioned burned in her mind and having been the one sent into the forest she was hell bent on finding answers.

Her thoughts were interrupted by the howl rising into the night, she sighed. She had spent one night already in the forest listening to that howl being carried on the breeze and all the while getting further away. The Hunter kept hoping that it was another answering the call and not that her prey was, as she feared becoming more distant. This was her last chance to not only slay the beast, if there was indeed a beast to slay, but to find answers to the burning questions that had led her to the forest in the first place.

The moon was just reaching its apex, which at this time of year meant that there was only a couple of hours left before dawn and once the soft light began to filter through the forest her chance would be gone. She would have to wait until the evening to pick up the trail again. Local folklore told how the beast only came out during the full moon and left no trace, not even after three nights. It was as if it was supernatural; a ghost. It was already the second night of the full moon's three-day cycle and the Hunter had made good ground She would neither waste the moonlight, nor would she return cowed, branded mad, or become enslaved. The fabled beast that cursed the women of the village would be revealed and defeated once and for all. She would return with its head for all to see. It would be proof that her wild nature and rebellious behaviour was a gift that could benefit all as opposed to something that needed to be cured or punished.

Another hour had passed before the she felt the first prickle through her body that something was amiss. The wind brought a sour tang with it and the wood did not feel as empty as it had done earlier. She was fully aware that she was now the one being hunted and that she would have to think quickly in order to not give herself away.

She continued following the trail, but more cautiously, heading towards a safer place on higher ground. This she hoped would not only protect her, but perhaps give her a better view of both her hunter and her prey. Moving slowly and purposefully the Hunter continued following the trail, dipping to the ground every thirty paces or so to check for markers; paw prints, droppings, scraps of fur, food or anything else. She knew it was a risky call, but she hoped it would buy her a little more time in order to work out who was stalking her.

She headed for the Tor; a rocky outcrop of giant boulders tumbled into a pile by an ancient glacier as if they were marbles. There she could find small, but high up places where one could hide. Taking a steady breath and dropping to a crouch the Hunter bowed her head and closed her eyes, allowing her other senses to heighten. The dank odour resembled moss on a cave wall, mingled with a sickly musk, she felt the dry panting and heard the soft crunch of leaves underfoot. Or more precisely under-feet! She worked out there were at least three hounds, that were less than a hundred yards away and judging by the lack of human voices they were unleashed, and master-less. The Hunter needed to be close enough to the Tor to outrun them in less time than it would take for the pack to catch her up; her heartbeat quickened at the thought. Whether the dogs heard her heart pounding, or whether they smelt the fear was hard to determine but the long low growl, that rumbled through her ribcage told her time was of the essence.

She grasped the hem of her cloak, pulling it high enough, so as not to trip and taking a firm grip on the handle of her sword, the Hunter shifted her weight ready to sprint.

Another growl rolled out from the shadow; the hounds were gaining ground. It had to be now otherwise the hounds would flank and close in. She closed her eyes, took a deep breath and swallowed hard, before opening them and running for all she was worth. She was nimble and surefooted over the uneven floor of the forest, leaping ditches and vaulting fallen branches. She knew this place, it was her sanctuary; every bank, every dyke, every fallen oak, and every stream.

The Elders had always said spending too much time in the wood was unnatural, that it would lead to an inner wildness and in turn forsake the protection of the village.

The Hunter did not care. The forest was sacred, it was alive; the wind whispered to her through the trees, while the streams beautiful song captivated her, lifting her spirit when she was down, and the rocky tor offered shelter when needed. The forest offered its own protection to those who loved it. If there was a supernatural beast that prowled it each full moon; sometimes wolf, sometimes human, that so callously broke and shamed so many of her sisterhood, then she would find it and bring its reign of terror to an end by delivering the beasts' head, while wearing its still bloody pelt.

The Hunter's concentration faltered as her mind wandered to her glorious victory, briefly forgetting the slavering dogs that were growing ever closer. She lost her footing, slipping on the rotting mulch and tumbled into a heap; her bow slid off her shoulder and her quiver spilled arrows that were to be lost among the bracken. The Tor, if it wasn't, certainly seemed a fair distance away and the shadows of the hounds were now visible among the trees. "Get up... Get up!" she willed herself still slightly winded from the fall, stumbling a little as she stooped to grab her fallen weapons, before racing off once more into the night. Her hood fell backwards, revealing a mass of unruly locks and fierce eyes. The silvery light of the full moon touched her skin, illuminating the hounds' quarry and the hunt quickened as she aimed for the Tor, running as fast as she could.

With her fist full of arrows and her cloak billowing behind her she ducked through the low branches and into a clearing. The full moon drenched the majestic form of the Tor stacked clumsily under the cold clear sky in front of her in silvery light. The copse was dense at the foot of the rock, but she knew the path and she hoped the hounds didn't. She didn't even break step as she hopped up onto the stone. The pack of dogs, their jaws slack with saliva burst through the tree line, she risked a glance over her shoulder to see them grind to a halt trying to navigate the dense thorny bushes; she could hear their hunger and she knew it wouldn't be long before they would break through the undergrowth and resume their chase. She was right. Moments later they were only feet away. They slowed and fanned out to flank her on either side. She kept going, each stride steeper and higher, as they followed her, first onto the low stones that poked through the earth, gaining distance as they climbed. The contrast of the hard, stone surface compared to the soft forest floor was an immediate advantage to the hounds and before long they were snapping at her heels. But still she climbed.

She could hear the howl of her prey in the distance but knew that she had no chance of resuming her hunt, not now, not while she herself was being hunted.

A hound caught the corner of her cloak in its sharp teeth and shook its head vigorously leaning back on its haunches tugging at her determined to pull her from the rock. She could see the bloodlust in its eyes. It was a look she knew well. She had seen it in her own eyes only the night before. She slipped slightly, just managing to kick out, connecting the toe of her boot squarely on its jaw; whimpering it rolled away, threads of fabric still lacing its mouth. Using the momentum of the kick she tried desperately to swing herself up onto a ledge out of their reach but to no avail. She slipped slightly and came face to face with the hounds. She gripped her sword tighter than ever, determined not to be their prey and a fleeting thought passed through her mind; 'Could this have been the fate of those before her?'

She heard the howl of the wolf she had been stalking. He seemed closer now, but so many thoughts were racing through her head that it was impossible to really be sure of anything. She was determined to stand her ground, however futile; she would not go down without a fight!

Thrashing at the hounds with her sword, the howl which had been growing ever closer was now clearly visible.

He was her size, if not larger and she was petrified. His large canines glinted in the moonlight as they dripped saliva onto the cold ground before her. She froze, unable to move. It became apparent that she had grossly underestimated her prey, as she witnessed the fury that followed as wolf and hounds fought only inches away from her. The fierce clashing of teeth and claws seemed to go on forever and though she was unharmed, she was unsure of the best course of action; to run or remain as still as she could. She chose the latter. Eventually, the injured hounds fled, whimpering into the night and the wolf lay bleeding at her feet.

Now was her chance. She could either leave the villagers demon wolf for dead or finish him and return triumphant as had been the original plan. Her heart was still pounding with fear and adrenaline surged through her as she tentatively edged close enough to look into his eyes, hoping to see the menacing evil that had terrorized so many before her, but instead, the moonlight revealed what appeared to be tears. She ventured nearer, captivated by the unending depth, she stared into the abyss. The Hunter sensed within him the same wild spirit that lived within her and as his eyes burned deep into her soul, she knew that there was no hiding her true nature and that he was fully aware it had been him that she was stalking through the forest.

But now as he lay helpless, she felt no hatred towards him, and no longer wondered about him, instead her curiosity was peaked, and different thoughts now raced through her mind. Was he? The wolf, and for that matter, was she? Not so much cursed but blessed with a freedom of spirit beyond the villager's comprehension, and what of those who had gone before her? What did they or didn't they know? What were they afraid of? Had they too been chased by hounds? And had *they* taken the time to discover the wolf's inner beauty? Hell! Did they even see the wolf? Or were they simply afraid of what lay in the forest? Or maybe they were just afraid of their own true nature. And the most compelling question of all… Where was the wolf the rest of the month? Or even, come the break of day?

She wouldn't have long to find out as there was only a couple of hours left till daybreak.

She had no wish to injure this creature, she wanted only to help him, after all he had saved her from the hounds, and it was if she could hear the voice of his heart whispering to her.

She lit a fire, partially to keep warm, the night as short as it was, had developed a chill in the air, but mostly to keep the hounds away; fire can be an excellent weapon. She tended his wounds as best she could and shared what little food she had, and in return she felt his companionship. And eventually, with only an hour till daybreak she curled up beside the wolf. The warmth from his body felt good and although she desperately wanted to stay awake, within minutes she was asleep.

She had no idea how long she slept for, but she awoke to a new sense of loneliness. She knew he would return tonight and this time she would discover once and for all the mystery that surrounded both him and the annual 'Howling.' She would search all night for the wolf if she had to; not as Hunter and prey but as kindred spirits.

As the third night drew closer, she knew that returning to the village was not an option, not now, not ever! Shades of red and orange blazed across the sky as the sun set on the third and final night, silhouetting the forest as darkness grew ever closer.

The wind gently rustled through the trees and she caught

the first faint hint of his scent. She knew he was close by and for the first time she felt safe. As his scent grew stronger, excitement surged up through her body and she felt the howl rise from deep within. And she knew she would be forever wild!

Based on an original song written and performed by Esme Knight and featured as a duet with Martin Jackson on the Forever Wild album (Produced by Josh Elliott (JGE Studios))

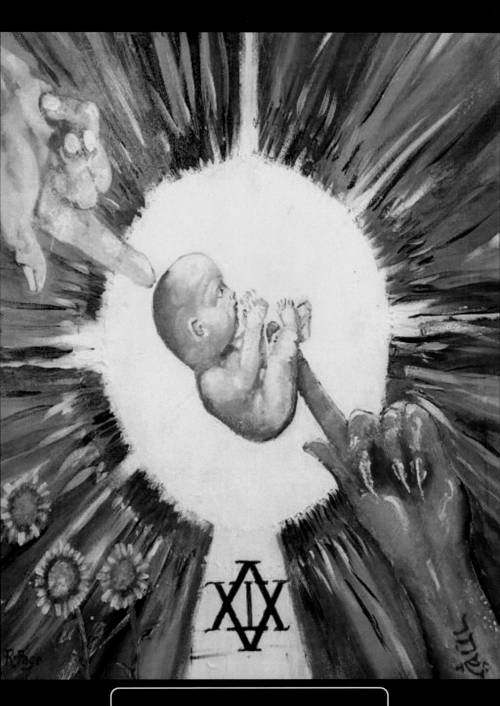

XIX THE SUN

THE SUN
Nineteen Circles - Richard K Page

The duty of the Sun begins at dawn and ends at dusk, although for the Sun himself, dusk and dawn are an entwined melody of perpetual inseparable moments, constant and unchanging. For him, every moment is both dawn and dusk as he gazes upwards into his skies somewhere towards the Earth, of which he has a keen interest. He regarded it as slightly more interesting than the other planets. Upwards of course as being spherical, downwards will always be the place behind his focal attention.

One particular moment between the other less remarkable "other moments" on the now risen Earth, the child suddenly realised that they were. They "were" in every sense of the word "were" so to speak. This at the time was a frustratingly difficult notion for the child, as the word "were" wasn't yet incorporated into his vocabulary, in-fact no words at all had as yet formed his lexicon, and so the child decided to make one up, a means of expressing that he was indeed "were" and he would express that to anyone who may be interested and to anybody and all that would listen.

Being unfamiliar with how much lung capacity he had as yet accumulated and how much of a stretch was the optimal amount to assign to the vocal cords, in order to make the air contract and expand into the vibrations of energy that he was about to share with the universe; he blasted out a sound whose wake would forever outwardly expand into an ever-diminishing substance of itself. Without caution he simply threw this spark of materialised brain flux out there into the yonder, regardless of consequence. Being quite the amateur at the whole conveying thoughts through this unfamiliar medium of sound malarkey, his "were" came out a somewhat shocking, but not an altogether too shabby "Waaaaaaaahhhhrrrree", which in hindsight, he was actually, quite pleased with. "Not too far away," he thought despite not having the words "not too far away." Either a language of pure thought without form was already present in his mind and in essence the general concept of a very near hit was pleasing to him, or some semblance of predetermined process and construction of thought was programmed into him from wherever he was; before he "were." Regardless, he decided to make several attempts again very soon.

Coincidentally, one would think if you don't believe in a grander scheme of purpose, it was just at that moment that he experienced his very first ever sight of light. "Well that's new" he would've thought if he had those words also, but despite his lack of verbosity it was new to him all the same, and he knew it was new. Therefore, one would think, "knew" is simply a reinforced post experience "new." Isn't it weird that we don't know what is new until we now know what we knew isn't new anymore? For the boy, this was his very own personal dawn to take tautological phrases to the Nth degree, a dawn which he shared with one of the Sun's many moments of perpetual dawns.

The Sun at the time was also busy being dawn to another portion of the Earth's inhabitants, and dusk to yet another. It saw no reason to interrupt this busy schedule of being in an eternal dichotomy of polarising states of expression, to two different sides of the world just to correct them into being aware that one thing can be the opposite of what you perceive it to be based on your perception of it, rather than its true expression. Of course, the child would eventually reason similar logic, but it would be a long time before he got bored enough to consider such matters.

The Sun however, already had a very long time. And with that, the Sun in his little section of consciousness was far too busy and self-absorbed to pay attention to this one child having a similar selfish moment of personal realisation to consider that there may be something more than the oblivion of nihility in the universal expanse of all in which one tiny spark of a neuron in its vast closed system of infinite space had become self-aware. "Did the child become aware or did yet another part of this universe become aware?" The Sun thought, "damn it now I'm beginning to pay attention to it" he also thought or rather he shouted, "in light," because that's how stars shout don't you know?

The Sun in some quarters, as well as being dusk and dawn, was also playing God, the big G, to most of the inhabitants of the Earth. Which was probably why he favoured it; he did so love the flattery. So, he made sure that she wasn't too hot or too cold unlike the other, less interesting planets, just so he could keep them little naïve guys alive. You see, on the one hand it was delivering a beautiful, warming respite to some of the otherwise colder northern regions favoured by the Earths inhabitants; melting the caps and crowns of the mountains which softened their icy hearts and poured into the lifeblood of fresh water, which are driven by the desire of elements to ultimately find eternal rest. This, in turn flowed downwards to the body of green hills and vales which lay in the emerald expanses beneath. In these regions, he was a much-loved God of beneficence. In songs and legend, he was the epitome of love and light. All life was bountiful in his gaze, and all those that worshipped him were blessed with eternal life and glory. Yes, this land was indeed the divine chosen lands and people were favoured by their beloved God.

Not so much for those further down south on the equatorial band of the Earth, which was over emphasised by her rotund waistline. Here ironically, where the Earth was at her fattest, the pickings were not so bountiful. Here the Sun was considered a vengeful god, intent on drying out the lands and turning them into dust. Woe betide anyone who dared to question his supreme and judgemental rule of the unfettered clear blue skies where no clouds could form. The rivers ran dry, the fauna and flora could not be found as the Sun must've been very angry and was punishing the people in these lands for their wicked ways. Indeed, their water was turned to salt. This was pretty much the way the world worked.

XIX

The further nineteen times that the Earth had annoyingly buzzed around the Sun's head, went mostly unnoticed in the grand scheme of things when compared to the other four-point-two-billion times it had previously done exactly the same spiralling dance. It was by now one would have no doubt, a fairly regular occurrence unmarred other than by the occasional visitor to the house. The whole system was running like clockwork. Clockwork being a mechanism that hadn't arrived in the system just yet, but you can rest assured that the person who invented it would base it on the fine example set by the Earth and its timely pirouette. It was nothing like in the early days when all the other planets were jostling for their position and making allegiances with other planets and moons for their space in this house of Sol.

The Earth as it happens, lucked out tremendously or drew the short straw depending on which way you look at it when it comes to finding the sweet spot. I say that because as it happens, though it had managed to find a spot conveniently nestled between too-hot and too-cold to support life, it was actually the case that the Sun was just not shouting that much at her, or ignoring her either; and that it regulated itself to keep her happy, wasn't luck at all, if she had been further away, he would've just shouted a little louder.

What made the Earth really lucky, was that she had managed to grab a fairly well-balanced selection of the four cardinal and classical elements: fire, air, water and earth, with the latter being the primary and namesake of this mishmash of a planet. All of these things made life an unlikely, but all the same inevitable feature of Mother Earth, who liked to be called Gai.

In the boy's comparatively short life however, those nineteen years had seen some quite remarkable changes. Over that time, the boy had developed his vernacular and his ability to form those words into spoken coherent instructions and expressions quite effectively. He was no longer, by any sense of the word, a child either. At some point, which wasn't really dictated by the number of orbits the Earth had done around the Sun, but more the experience of life and the approach towards its ongoing revelations, Chiyik had become a man and apparently been given a name, although that event was quite early in the whole process; one which I could have easily skipped over.

Chiyik, pronounced "Jake," was a now a nineteen-year- old man, who lived on a large peninsula halfway up the northern hemisphere in the somewhat temperate zone. His people had a great reverence for the environment they had found themselves in and had just reached one of the earliest stages in evolution where it was attempting to distinguish itself from all the other animals. It had familiarised itself with using objects in its surroundings to make its life easier, but most importantly it had conceived the idea that if the tool did not exist, then it could be fashioned out of other stuff, which was really a huge leap in that endeavour. In fact, it was a huge leap in all endeavours except leaping, but don't worry, springs, rubber heels and nano fibres would eventually be invented to enhance leaping, but that would occur outside of this story.

Mankind had also learned to use other animals. Many protested, but mankind isn't used to taking no for an answer. It left "taking no for an answer" to the lesser creatures, which were inevitably going to die out for being too damn reasonable when confronted with the proposition "you either adapt and fit in or get the hell off this planet." Animals, being less able to enforce their opinion since they had not yet realised that thoughts could be converted into soundwaves which allowed others to estimate the validity of your consciousness; animals remained for the most part literally dumb, and so if they did have any objection to being eaten or hunted it was their fault as they didn't speak up! Well that's how mankind saw it. Not only that, they didn't luck out with physicality either. I mean, most animals can fight with their hands, feet or teeth, but rarely all. Man however, not only had all three but would often pick up other stuff and hit things with that too. The underappreciated act of "picking stuff up," was man's greatest achievement in the early days. If we had hoofs, we'd have been fucked!

Despite seeing man do this for millions of years with varying success, no other creature it seems was smart enough to think "that's a good idea, I could do that too" and instead just queued up behind a long line of weird duck faced cows and long-legged mice that were destined for early extinction. Regardless of mans' exemplary efforts at intimately showing animals how to kill bigger stronger other animals with tools, animals were still confused over the whole simplicity of the tool to use them effectively. Well, except a weird water badger-like thing, who liked to lay rocks on his belly and crack eggs while floating on his back down streams. It won't be long, before they realise that if they make the rock sharp, they can start to wear other animal skins as fur. Maybe because they already have fur, they hadn't thought it a useful addition.

Chiyik, had mastered the Horse. Another one of man's early great schemes, the idea to save himself having to use his own legs. However well-proportioned and adaptive our legs were when compared to the waddles of a penguin for example. We quickly decided to abandon the use of them and to watch other people walking instead on our later arriving telly boxes. The horse

143

for his even-better-than-ours legs, quickly gained favour with man, who for the most part promised not to eat him like he did all the other animals in return for his equestrian service. Man also promised that the horse was fed and not whipped as long as it kept doing quite heavy work for him. Given the limited options, the horse begrudgingly conceded… "damn the hooves, why if I had opposable thumbs, I'd…"

Chiyik called his horse Aeos (pronounced Yes). Aeos was a fine white stallion and the envy of all of Pangia, where Chiyik lived. One day after a long ride in the fields, something Chiyik did every day to look over his lands and make sure all was flourishing as expected, Chiyik was contemplating the four elements, and how they had so beautifully combined to create the perfection he found in the world. He looked at the river flowing and compared it to the blood in his veins, and as he did so, he plucked a single daisy from the company of the lush green grass. Picking its petals and blowing them and their seeds into the wind "where life is lost, life is renewed he thought," such is the cycle of all things. Then he considered the wind, he took in a deep breath and considered the air outside whose fragrance and taste was so divine that he could not distinguish it from his own preferences, for it was tasteless and smell-less, yet with every breath, he knew he was truly feeling life. As he drew that which was outside inwards, he realised that which was without is also within, and which is above is also below. He realised that air was his favourite of consummations, in-fact he couldn't imagine life without it.

He plucked another Daisy as he exhaled, returning air to the world, in the same way that he believed his spirit would return to the heavens, from which it must've arrived here on Earth at the end of his cycle of life. For a short while, "the air was him" he thought. The air he absorbed was a part of "the stuff" which was making up who he was. All things small could be considered just a microcosm of the larger all. The air seemed to be a spirit that loved him from the inside, much like he was inside something that was an extension of him: he and the world were one, he was just a part of it, like the daisy and the grass made the field; a single blade was as much the field as the field itself and a single person was the world.

The third element he considered was earth as he saw the seed return to the mother who would nurture it back into a new independent life and as he plucked another daisy, he looked at its form and marvelled how such beauty could be.

It was then that he realised that the air and the rivers were without form, but were mailable to that of their hosts, as to some extent was fire; the fourth and final element for which another daisy was picked. But earth, the earth was the form, he concluded, his body was of the earth and his spirit was of the air, and all could be considered all.

The fire was his desire, consuming and driven. It was thought without form, forever seeking the other elements like air and earth for fuel. Quenching this fire, was water, his blood; moving and empowering his changes to his environment. Like the rivers that carved their way from the mountains to the sea, he could carve the life he desired by shaping the terrain of his future, which left him only musing back to earth as his body and air as his spirit, both which he shared with his environment. Aeos ate some grass.

All these things he shared with the Sun, and he took comfort in knowing that he was a part of all these things, and all things no matter where he stood shared common dispositions, which simply meant that they only appeared to be something other than ourselves, but in reality, we are all just a tiny part of something much bigger; isolated by our points of view. It was then that Chiyik truly became aware once again, but in a new knew way, and so, he cried "Waaaaaaaahhhhrrrree." And the Sun looked up at Chiyik and shouted back in a scream of light, and for

145

a moment they knew each other were as one. Aeos neighed, but Chiyik didn't know if that was in agreement, or to the adverse of the moment. Whatever, the three were soul mates for sure.

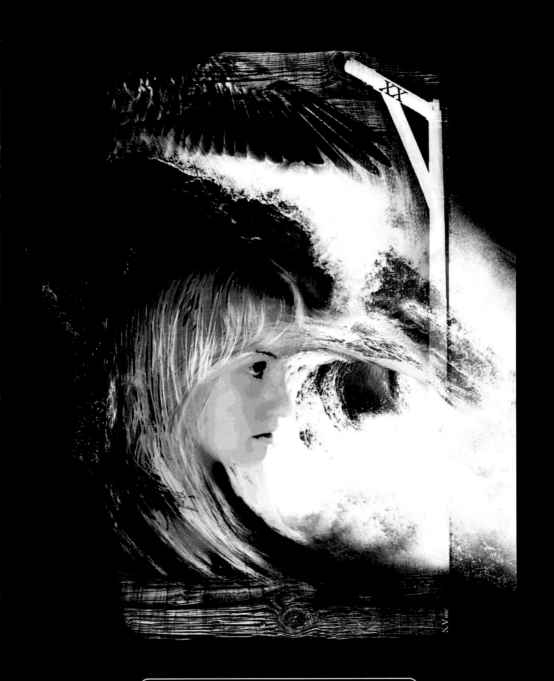

XX JUDGEMENT

JUDGEMENT
Elimanzer and the Captain - Mark Vine

Edith Trevitt, now sure that she had the full and undivided attention of her audience, leaned slowly forwards in her chair and said in a broad Dorset accent, *"It's a tragedy to be certain, but not one that I didn't see comin,"*

The assembled ladies of the town all nodded and squawked in chicken-like agreement.

"And o'course, he were a man o' Poole originally, not a native of Dorchester at all" she added, and then more gravely still, *"And you know what they say about Poole men don't yer? 'If Poole were a fish pool and the men o' Poole fish, there'd be a pool for the Devil, and fish for His dish.'*

The ladies gasped, staring wide-eyed, and one evoked God's help to protect them from the obvious evil all around. Mrs Trevitt continued.

"And 'im bein' here in the first place was born out o' tragedy mind. His wife and pretty young daughter, who 'e idolised, both drowned at sea, and on 'is own ship as well, God rest their souls. And it were the child's birthday the day it happened." She sighed long and hard, *"Well I mean to say, it would play on any man's mind wouldn't it, any man with a heart...even a Poole man... Yes, cut him deep to the bone it did, deep to the bone. 'Tis said that's why he moved to Dorchester, so that he wouldn't have to look at the sea ever again."*

This was the third 'performance' that Mrs Trevitt had given since the trial and some of the ladies there assembled, were on their second hearing of events, such was the interest generated by the imminent demise, by public execution, of her ex-employer, Captain Richard Gleed. The sentence was due to be carried out on the very next day, October 31st, 1855.

"I mean, who ever heard of a sea-captain who was afraid of the sea?" she laughed, then shaking her head, concluded, "No, tragedy born out o' tragedy, that's what it was, and I should know because no-one was closer to 'im than me... No one!" She said with added emphasis.

She sipped her cup of tea and contentedly eyed the gathering as they predictably agreed with her once more, then went on.

"And what with this queer business which 'e used to get up to in the countryside hereabouts, well, 'twas bound to set tongues a waggin' wasn't it though. Messin' about in them muddy old ploughed fields searchin' for them dirty old bits of I don't know what, the way he did. He told me once they were things that the Romans and other Ancients who lived in Dorset in times gone by had fashioned hundreds o' years before. Coins and brooches and stuff, he said they were, but it all looked like rubbish to me, and I told 'im so, all green an' dirty. Still he seemed to enjoy it, and it kept 'is mind off t'other business with his family I s'pose."

Again, she paused, and in a low secretive voice added, "And really, it could be said that his doin's in them fields was the start of his downfall. After all, didn't he meet 'her' first off when he was muckin' about in one." The women all nodded again, open-mouthed, some with teacups motionlessly poised midway between lap and lips.

"I remember that mornin' as if it were yesterday. I got to his house at about seven o' clock as usual to do 'im a bit o' breakfast and clean up, but he was already up an' about.

'I'm off to Maiden Castle,' says he. Quite jolly he was, for a man that was settin' off on the road to ruin, if he but only knew it." She sniffed loudly. "Well, that's 'ow come he met her wasn't it...Elimanzer."

A disdainful moan blew around the small parlour like an easterly wind, and the women all glanced at each other knowingly. Mrs Trevitt continued.

"Apparently, he stopped off at this farmhouse near Maiden Hill, to enquire if anyone there fancied earnin' themselves a shillin' or two helpin' him for the day in searchin' for them bits of metal he collected, two pairs of eyes bein' better than one as they say. Well, the woman there, Elimanzer's mother, told him that there was no one, except her brother, who was all but blinded in the Crimea and had no more brains than a turnip. Then she suggests her, 'Elimanzer.' 'A child's eyes bein' as good as any and better than most,' she said.

"Anyway, as soon as he lays eyes upon her, that was that. She turned his head y'see, right from the off. All he knew, poor man, was that he was staring at the very image of his own dead daughter, her that drowned off Portland in a squall thirteen years before."

Mrs Trevitt shook her head, slowly and sadly.

"I'll tell you all now...when he got back that evening, he was a changed man. I've never seen a body so altered or distracted as 'e was then. It was as if a spell 'ad been put on him, and you all know by who."

The women gasped aloud once more and with bated breath sat transfixed, waiting for the next revelation to unfold, even though they all knew what was coming next, having heard the testimony in the courtroom the week before and read all about it in the local paper.

"Changed he was, and the next day he offered her a maid's job, tellin' the mother that he was so impressed with her diligence in the fields, that he was willin' to give her a start in his own house here in Dorchester. And the wage he promised to pay her was such that the mother could scarcely refuse him."

Mrs Trevitt had now reached her favourite part of the whole performance. Her bottom lip began to quiver and in a weepy, simpering and well-rehearsed voice she declared,

"When I think of all them years I've faithfully served 'im.

All the favours I've done 'im, and never once did he ever suggest that I move in with him to make my life any easier. All those years of him rattlin' about on his own in that gert big old house like a tomtit on a quarter of horseflesh." She produced a handkerchief, dabbed at her tearful eyes with it and loudly blew her nose, before declaring. *"Still, I'm not one to complain."*

A moment later, and quite recovered she went on Imperiously. *"Now I'm not one to cast aspersions either, as you all know but, I knew from the off that there was somethin' queer about that girl. Her name for a start, ELIMANZER BOWDITCH! What sort o'name is that for a Christian soul to bear? And as for that cock n'bull story she told about that huge brute of a dog of 'ers that she refused to be parted from, rescuin' her from a pond she fell in to as a nipper...well if that ain't suspect I don't know what is. Hulkin' great black beast, went for me it did once, when I slapped her face for droppin' a jug o' milk, it near ripped my throat out...That's when I told him, it's either me or her. 'Course, you know the rest. Took her side against me didn't he, so I 'anded him my notice, there and then. Now I ain't one to mark another down as a witch, but you all know what them country folk be like."*

Again, moans of derision filled the room and one woman croaked,

"You should've hung up a bullock's heart studded with thorns and pins, no witch alive can cross a threshold past a charm like that," and several women nodded.

"See what I didn't know then was, that she was actually born on the very night that his own dear daughter drowned," said Mrs Trevitt. *"And when he found that out, well, that was that. Nothing on earth was going to persuade him that she wasn't his own sweet child come back from a watery grave t' be with him again."*

"The good Lord works in mysterious ways, his wonders to perform," echoed a meek voice from the back of the room.

151

Mrs Trevitt frowned and said sharply, *"Indeed he does dear, but I don't think he intended me to lose my position* through it. No, you mark my words, there's somethin' darker *afoot here, somethin' not fashioned in heaven above, or anywhere near it."*

Pointing at nobody in particular she added, *"And I can hold my head up in the street and stand by my actions. Yes, I admit it, I did march straight round to that little whelp's mother, and I told her to her face, right in front of that half-blind, half-daft uncle, and Elimanzer's brother, God rest 'is soul, exactly what was going on there with the pair of 'em, or at least, what folk hereabouts said was goin' on. You know how some people will gossip. But how was I t' know that the brother had a fearsome temper on 'im and would go straight round there like a bull at a gate to 'ave it out with the Captain. I mean to say, I had to show 'im where the house was didn't I? or he might have took it out on me too"* ...

Mrs Trevitt became emotional again and shook her head. *"He was a lovely lookin' young man her brother, tall, dark, and strong as an ox. Who would 'ave thought that a man more than twice his age would 'ave bettered 'im like that? There's only one answer to it, the Captain 'ad the Devil in 'im. Soon as that brother said he was takin' the girl back 'ome, he flew at him like a thing possessed, and snapped 'is neck like a dry twig"* ...

***

The next morning was cold, and overnight rain had turned the ground around the gallows to slush. The crowd booed and hissed as Captain Gleed was led out and mounted the scaffold. He stood unbowed at the rail as the charge and sentence was read.

Again, the crowd grew restless, but fell silent as Gleed began to speak his last words.

"You all have your opinions of me." he sneered, and, staring straight at Edith Trevitt positioned prominently at the

152

front of the throng, added, *"Some of you had too many opinions, and expectations."*

At this there were a few ripples of knowing laughter, and Mrs Trevitt frowned hard. The condemned man continued.

"But what a man has lost, then found again and made good on, is easier to part with a second time... I hereby declare now before all of you and almighty God that I leave my wealth, my house and all its contents, to Miss Elimanzer Bowditch of Winterborne Monkton" ... The crowd gasped in shocked amazement...

Then with one last blood chilling glare at his former housekeeper, he turned and nodded to the hangman. *"Get on with man and do your duty"*

Mrs Trevitt watched smugly as the rope was placed around the prisoner's neck. Gleed stared unflinchingly ahead. The pain and affront that she imagined had been done to her was at last about to be put to rights. Edith Trevitt smirked, but was momentarily distracted from her triumph by a figure which suddenly appeared in an upstairs window of the prison behind the scaffold. She stared hard at it, as it, stared back at her.

Straining her eyes, all she could see now was that face, that all too familiar young face, nothing else seemed to exist at all as it began to completely transfix her in its mesmerising gaze. She wanted to point at it and tell those around her about the figure, but she simply couldn't move, couldn't do anything but look straight ahead. Even the execution seemed to fade away in front of her. She heard the last mumblings of the clergyman, the trapdoor open and the body fall and twist in vain, but could not look upon it, and, as the crowd held its breath, she too now began to feel an intense pressure around her own throat.

As Gleed writhed in restricted flight, Edith Trevitt felt her own windpipe being slowly but relentlessly crushed. Choking, she desperately clawed in vain at her own throat, but to no avail, and still she was compelled to stare at the face in the window, the awful, vengeful face that stared back at her in its own, empty, pitiless gaze, with a countenance that seemed to pierce right through to her very soul.

Then, as Gleed's body finally ceased its doomed struggle for life, Edith Trevitt, wide-eyed, fell down dead, face first in the mud before the scaffold.

A thin smile creased the face of the diminutive figure in the window. She reached down a hand and patted the head of the large black panting dog which sat obediently at her side... Then she turned and disappeared from view.

XXI THE WORLD

THE WORLD

The Gypsy and the Stranger Diane Narraway

'Come in dearie...I can sense you have an exciting future ahead'

No doubt she had used the same line on dozens of people that day, and undoubtedly some of them, like me, had fallen for it. It's not that I'm especially stupid or that I actually believe the Gypsy spiel (if indeed she is a real gypsy). What I am is bored! I'm walking along the sea front past all the arcades with a pocket full of wages and no idea what I want in life; no direction as such.

I am single and bored...I mentioned bored, didn't I? I need something fulfilling! Working as a waitress in a coffee shop is hardly exciting, challenging or even interesting. Clearly, when I took the job, which I did apply for, I had some romantic notion of meeting the man of my dreams. Instead, I have met several geriatrics from the local 'old folk's home' a few fishermen and those I refer to as the bingo crew; two fat ladies and a naughty forty all of which consume copious amounts of tea and cake amidst raucous laughter. Every, Monday an old man with a stick known as Norman (Normal Norman, we call him), comments as to how the naughty forty could make him a very happy man. Truth to tell, I don't know which is worse, the tediousness and the predictability or the fact that I even know any Bingo calls! Even more depressing is how I know them; various trips to Bingo with my Mother. Yes, my life is really that tragic

And so, here I am a fool and her money soon to be parted, for yet another 5 minute's worth of old lady speak. I know it's a take whatever she says with a pinch of salt scenario, but I can't help but secretly hope that she has some genuine gift and that I really do have an exciting future ahead of me, and it's not as if it could be less exciting.

'Right then dear, I need you to shuffle these and focus on your question'

I dutifully, almost mechanically obeyed; picked up the cards and began to shuffle. I hadn't actually got a question, and quite honestly the only things running through my mind were...how little she looked like my idea of a gypsy fortune teller. She was old, very wrinkly and bore much more resemblance to a squashed teabag, and no resemblance whatsoever to what's her face in the Bond Movie, or any of the other glamorous raven-haired Romany beauties I had pictured. In fact, the only resemblance she had was her cards. The head scarf which sat slightly lopsided on her head and the ridiculous over-sized chav hoops in her ears just made her look more grotesque and very fake.

Like I said I shuffled the cards with no inkling of any question. I guess if she had looked the part or at least if the tacky imitation Romany caravan had looked slightly less plastic and wood veneer, I might have been able to consider taking it a little bit seriously. I think one question may have been a bit optimistic: I started each day wondering how to get a better job, whether to go back to college, wondering if I would meet someone tall dark and handsome, or just the usual short, chubby and too damned old!! I'd spend a good twenty minutes trying to decide what to wear. And pay day was even worse...God knows how many questions I ask myself on that day and sat in this nasty little excuse of a caravan opposite tea-bag face, I was asking myself why I hadn't just carried on walking like the rest of the passers-by.

But I didn't, so I may as well make the most of it, best of it...or at least have a funny story to tell at work. So, I sat there, poker faced as she reeled of the cards.

'Aaaah' she said all mysteriously with a long pause. So long in fact, I wondered if she was going to add anything else at all or if this was thirty quid even more wasted than I had originally thought! But eventually she did continue, passing off the extreme pause as "Communicating with her spiritual guides." I wasn't entirely sure that my cynical input would be welcome at this point, so I stayed quiet and let her continue.

'The Queen of Swords. You have many questions and little direction…you are seeking fulfilment, something more satisfying more…more challenging…' There's that pause again as she turns over the next card. And ok she may have been slightly right, but we are only one card in, and there can't be any one on the planet who doesn't want something "more in their life"

A few cards later, I was paying more attention. Perhaps I had misjudged Gypsy Rose Tea Bag, maybe she does have some sort of gift. She had seen my past, knew my job bored me rigid and that my mother was the closest person to me, my lack of social life and my "Billy no-mates" status. In fact, she said I was the saddest person she'd ever read for. She was definitely right on that one. I was sad in every sense of the word!

Although, I didn't need to part with thirty quid to be told all that…I already knew it.

'Your future does look brighter dear… You will meet a stranger… A man' at this point her voice deepened and became softer making her sound mysterious and all knowing.

'You will meet him very soon… He will be important to you…I can see travel…and water… It's all in the very near future…I sense it growing closer' She turned over the last card; it was the World, so she informed me. 'This is good…very good' she continued in her mysterious voice 'This means it will be the end of a chapter and the beginning of an adventure' her voice had become higher again but excited. 'See? See?' she exclaimed, re iterating it for me by tapping the card while still exclaiming excitably 'See? See?' all I could see was a naked woman with a sash round her holding a couple of batons. Surely, she wasn't about to tell me I was going to join a naked majorette troupe or become Miss World! So, no I didn't "See? … See?"

'The man, the travel, the water…it is a new chapter and it

will be so fortunate for you. It will bring you great fulfilment, a sense of completion…it will be wondrous'

Her excitement was a bit infectious and I couldn't help but feel a sneaky bit hopeful about the future, which was interrupted by the rasping,

'Thirty-quid please' I handed her the money undaunted by her voice returning to normal. Honestly, I hardly noticed the change in it and in my flush of optimism even the caravan seemed less tacky; perhaps all that alone was worth the thirty quid.

I left feeling a lot lighter than before and not just thirty quid lighter. I felt what my mother would refer to as blind optimism. Despite my new-found optimism, I still wasn't happy when I felt the first few drops of rain. Bloody weather! My worst fears were as always correct when the heavens opened and what began as an April shower turned into a complete deluge. Bloody typical!

Absolutely opposed to the idea of getting wet I headed for the bus stop, seriously hoping this wasn't the water the Old Mother Tea Bag had predicted; along with thoughts of how I may never see a cup of tea the same way, although I am not entirely sure whether it will make me smile or scowl. This I felt would largely depend on whether or not catching a bus in the rain was the travel and water she had predicted ten minutes ago.

By the time the bus arrived nearly half an hour later, not only had my mood plummeted, but the rain had become torrential and the traffic ridiculous. A rather overweight and bad-tempered driver allowed three people ahead of me on before shouting 'Sorry love…no room…you'll have to get the next one.'
"Oh great,"
I'm cold, wet and the idea of spending another half hour at the bus stop with the possibility of not getting on is just too much. Sod it! I'll get a taxi.

Of course, taxis were few and far between. It seemed the

weather had caused far more chaos than I had anticipated. I was forced to buy a newspaper just to hold over my head; it always works in the movies. Eventually, and sporting a very soggy newspaper a taxi pulled up.

'Where you headed?'

'13, Acacia Drive' I replied without looking up

'Okay, well, I'll take you if you ditch the paper...I'm not having that soggy thing in me cab'

'Whatever' I replied less than graciously and ditching the paper in a nearby bin.

'It works in the movies you know?'

'What does' his voice was calm, kinda soothing.

'The holding a newspaper over your head...they always do that when catching a New York cab in the rain'

'Perhaps, the rain in New York isn't as wet as ours'

'Nothings as wet as ours' I laughed catching a glimpse of his smile in the mirror.

'You might be right there' he laughed.

We must've only gone a few miles when he stopped.

'Why have you stopped?' My house was at least another five miles away. I wasn't sure whether I should be scared... Was this a wrong turn moment... Did I just watch too much shit on DVD and so on.

'The roads closed look' he said interrupting my train of thought; which was probably a good thing, as I was only moments away, from spraying the Fem Fresh I kept in my bag in his eyes. I followed his pointing and yep sure enough the sign said road closed. A police officer came over and suggested we either turn back or find an alternative route.

'I know a back route I can take... It's a bit rough in places and a bit out the way but I'll only charge you the same amount as if I'd gone this way... What d'you reckon? Shall we give it a go?'

I thought for a moment. One the one hand he had a nice smile was really quite cute and didn't look like a serial killer, but on the other hand, I've seen *American Psycho* and *Ted Bundy*. The swaying decider was neither of these things it was the incessant rain which was literally throwing it down.

'Yeah sure, why not?'

'D'you wanna ride shotgun… I promise I don't bite'

Did he have to use the word shotgun?…

'Er yeah ok' I couldn't have sounded more nervous if I'd tried.

Fortunately, I had jeans and trainers on otherwise I would probably have stayed put. Instead, I reached the front passenger seat by way of a very undignified manoeuvre which involved climbing over the centre console, catching my foot and somehow ending up on my back with my legs in the air and my shoe on the floor in the back. It involved a further undignified manoeuvre to correct my position followed by groping around on the floor in the back with my arse stuck up in the air in order to reach my trainer. And yeah, I could hear my cabbie, saviour, serial killer laughing throughout the whole sorry event. Finally, I corrected myself, returning my trainer to its rightful position on my foot.

'Are you OK now. Shall we go?'

'Yes' I managed in a very disgruntled tone.

An uncomfortable silence followed. It wasn't until, we were, I believe from the satnav, only a couple of miles from home when we stopped suddenly.

'What's happened? Why have we stopped? … What's going on?'

'We've hit a dead end'

'How? … You said you knew this route' My life was flashing before me. It just goes to show how tedious my life was when the first thing into my head was the dodgy Tea Bag faced fortune teller's words. And to some extent she had been right it had involved water and travel, and assuming he isn't a serial killer (the jury is as yet out on that one), the cabbie is kinda cute;

definitely fanciable. Could this be termed as an adventure. Again, only if I don't die!!

'I'm sorry I thought I did...but it must've changed since I last came up here...or my memory isn't as good as I thought. Don't worry I'll get you home dry if it kills me.' Oh, fantastic now he's going to die as well. By home does he mean the afterlife. Oh, for goodness sake get a grip girl!

'I've got a flask of coffee if you'd like a cup...I always carry a spare cup just in case pretty half-soaked girls get in my cab.' He handed me the cup.

I take it and note the fact that he just called me pretty.

'Thank you'

It tastes sweet and as long as we are stuck here, I may as well take my chances with him...after all if I run, I'll only fall over it's torrential out there and I have no idea where I am.

'Hungry?'

He offers me a sandwich. A proper cheese and pickle doorstep type sandwich not one of those nasty packaged ones they sell in garages. For the first time I notice his eyes are as beautiful as his smile.

'When we finally get out of here and I get you home...d'you fancy going for a drink...or a bite to eat? You never know it might be fun...a bit of an adventure even'

Well, what could I say?